orca limelights

LEARNING THE ROPES

Monique Polak

ORCA BOOK PUBLISHERS

Library and Archives Canada Cataloguing in Publication

Polak, Monique, author
Learning the ropes / Monique Polak.
(Orca limelights)

Issued in print and electronic formats.
ISBN 978-1-4598-0452-4 (pbk.).—ISBN 978-1-4598-0453-1 (pdf).—
ISBN 978-1-4598-0454-8 (epub)

I. Title. II. Series: Orca limelights
PS8631.O43L43 2015 jC813'.6 C2014-906671-6
C2014-906672-4

First published in the United States, 2015
Library of Congress Control Number: 2014952059

Summary: Mandy is thrilled to spend the summer at a Montreal circus camp, but she is forced to face her fears when another aerialist is killed in a fall.

Orca Book Publishers is dedicated to preserving the environment and has printed this book on Forest Stewardship Council® certified paper.

Orca Book Publishers gratefully acknowledges the support for its publishing programs provided by the following agencies: the Government of Canada through the Canada Book Fund and the Canada Council for the Arts, and the Province of British Columbia through the BC Arts Council and the Book Publishing Tax Credit.

Cover design by Rachel Page
Cover photography by Ibon Landa

ORCA BOOK PUBLISHERS
PO Box 5626, Stn. B
Victoria, BC Canada
V8R 6S4

ORCA BOOK PUBLISHERS
PO Box 468
Custer, WA USA
98240-0468

www.orcabook.com
Printed and bound in Canada.

18 17 16 15 • 4 3 2 1

For Lauren Abrams,
the performer in our family, with love

One

A pile of suitcases blocks my way to the check-in counter.

"Some people!" a woman in front of me mutters—loud enough for the couple who have left their suitcases in our way to hear. The woman tugs on her little boy's hand and leads him around the suitcases. They duck under the cord (it's easy for the boy, but the woman groans) and get back in line.

I don't mind the suitcases. For me, they're something to play with.

I toss my backpack over them. It lands with a small thud on the other side. I plant the heel of my hand on the top suitcase, nice and steady. Then I get a little bounce going in my knees, and I flip into a handstand. Which takes me right over the suitcases.

The boy's mouth falls open.

He giggles when I turn to him and take a bow.

Mom has ducked under the cord. "That's my girl, always putting on a show," she says to no one in particular, but not unkindly.

Dad hasn't come to Vancouver International Airport to see me off. He's against my going to circus camp in Montreal. He's against all things circus. *You could get hurt, Mandy, and you know it. Accidents happen. Think about what happened to your grandpa. Are you even listening, Mandy?*

Mom's the one paying for circus camp, not to mention airfare and my room and board. She says a person needs to follow her dreams, even if there's a risk involved. Something tells me Mom's dream wasn't to do the billing for Dad's engineering company.

When I'm done checking in, I can feel Mom giving me a final look-over. I'm wearing my usual—comfortable jeans and a soft, black T-shirt. "You're looking at me like I'm a package you're about to put in the mail," I tell Mom.

She gives me a fierce hug. "A precious package," she whispers. "Text me as soon as you land."

Two weeks will be the longest I've ever been away from home.

"Thanks, Mom. For everything."

"Don't be angry at your dad," she says into my ear. "You know how hard this is for him."

The hug ends, and we're trying not to cry. Then we both gulp at the same time, which makes us laugh.

Mom rests her hand on my shoulder. "Get outta here, will ya?"

* * *

I'm too excited to pay attention as the flight attendant explains the emergency exits. In about six hours, I, Mandy Campbell, will be at the Montreal Circus College's Summer Circus Camp. *Each year, only twenty-five teenagers from around the world are accepted into this prestigious program.* If that sounds like an ad, it's because I memorized it from the brochure.

I need to stand out at circus camp. If I do, it'll improve my chances of being accepted into the

Montreal Circus College. If I make it into MCC and stand out there, chances are good I'll get a job with a real circus, maybe even Cirque de la Lune, the greatest, most famous circus ever.

Somewhere over the Rocky Mountains, I doze off. I dream I'm climbing the old oak tree in our backyard in North Vancouver. My arms and legs work together like an engine, propelling me up the trunk. When I reach the top, all I can see is blue sky—and the window to the attic, where my dad's home office is. The screen is open to let in the fresh air. Dad is hunched over his computer. "Daddy!" I call. "Look at me!" But he won't look up.

"Are you all right, dear?" the woman sitting next to me asks. I can feel her staring at my legs. I've fallen asleep with them up in the air, resting on the back of the seat in front of me.

"I'm fine. Thanks." I lower my legs, crossing them at the ankle the way my seat partner probably expects me to.

The flight attendant comes rattling down the aisle with the beverages cart. I'm reaching for my soda water when I notice a dark-haired girl in the window seat across the aisle. She's fallen asleep too.

Her legs are crossed in her lap, and her head has dropped so low it nearly skims the floor.

She's either some kind of double-jointed yogi or she's headed for circus camp too.

* * *

When I exit through the glass doors of Montreal's Pierre Elliott Trudeau International Airport, I spot a small woman with blond hair holding up a sign that says *MCC Summer Circus Camp.* The girl from the airplane is behind me, and we're both waving to the woman with the sign.

The woman's name is Suzanne. I'd guess from her muscular build that she's done circus too. "Mandy? Genevieve?" she says, looking from one of us to the other as if she is trying to figure out who's who. "Welcome to Montreal. Have you two already met?"

Genevieve is from Seattle. She's wearing a hot-pink crop-top and skintight yoga pants, not to mention way too much makeup for a plane ride. Her black eyeliner sweeps up at the outer corners of her eyes, and she must have on three coats of pink lip gloss.

I get a small pang in my chest when Genevieve tells me she's an aerialist too. I could use a friend—so what if she wears too much makeup and I don't touch the stuff?—but I also know how competitive circus camp is going to be. There will probably only be a spot at the Montreal Circus College for one star aerialist. And it had better be me.

Genevieve flips her long dark hair back. "I do tissu," she says.

Most girls who are aerialists do tissu, the circus term for aerial fabric.

For a second, Genevieve's eyes stay on my jeans. I can feel her judging me. "I climb rope," I tell her. If my hair were long enough, I'd flip it the way she keeps flipping hers. I can't help feeling superior. Sure, tissu is pretty and feminine—like Genevieve—but it's a cliché in the circus world.

Rope is so much cooler.

Two

My breath catches in my throat when Suzanne exits from the highway onto a street called Iberville. There, right in front of me, taking up nearly the whole front window of the van, is a giant blue-and-yellow-striped tent—the big top—and next to it, the Cirque de la Lune headquarters, the round building where Cirque performers train. I've seen this view in the brochure and on the Internet a thousand times, but now I'm here. *I've arrived.* I blink—twice—just to make sure this is really happening.

"Wow," Genevieve says, which is how I know she feels the same way.

Suzanne is the camp director. Camp takes place in the Montreal Circus College building.

Like everything else on this block in Montreal's north end, it's big, shiny and new. Tall tinted windows make it impossible to see what's happening inside. "That's because everyone is curious about the circus and what we do in here," Suzanne tells us.

Yeah, I think, everyone except my dad.

There's a concrete terrace outside the MCC building. Suzanne explains that there'll be a barbecue there tomorrow night to celebrate the start of camp.

After we get our security passes, Suzanne takes us up to the third floor, where the dorms are. For the next two weeks, a dozen girls will share one large bright room—and two bathrooms.

Bunk beds line the walls. "Since you're both climbers, I'm guessing you'll want the top bunks," Suzanne says. "Backpacks and suitcases go under the bottom bunks. We need to be sure there's room to walk. Let me show you the bathrooms."

There's so much to see—*la palestre*, the giant training studio where we'll have some of our classes and where we'll perform on the last day of circus camp; the smaller studios; the gleaming cafeteria where we'll have most of our meals. Finally, I realize I've forgotten to text my mom.

`Sorry, Mom,` I write to her. `Landed safe. Amazing here. Love u.`

I nearly add *Say hi to Dad for me*, but I decide against it. I haven't completely forgiven him for not coming to the airport to see me off.

For a second I remember what my mom said when she was hugging me goodbye: *You know how hard this is for him.* Dad's father was a stuntman in the movie industry. I never got to meet him, though it sounds like we'd have got along. Dad says Grandpa was a daredevil who wasn't afraid of anything. Unfortunately, he died on a movie set at the age of forty-two.

In a climbing accident.

Suzanne explains that the boys have a room at the other end of the third floor and two bathrooms of their own. Genevieve wants to know whether there's a plug for her blow-dryer in the girls' bathroom. "There's no way I can go around with frizzy hair," she tells Suzanne.

Other kids have been arriving all day. Some are delivered by their parents. Some come by bus or train. Suzanne tells us she'll go back to the airport after supper to collect another group.

Genevieve and I meet Hana, an acrobat from Korea. She looks like a porcelain doll, and her English isn't very good. Then there's Cécile, a tightrope walker from France, and Anastasia, a Russian trapeze artist. "I'm Anastasia Bershov," she tells us. She has a British accent and a handshake that leaves my fingers aching.

"Did you just say *Bershov*?" Genevieve asks.

"That's correct." Anastasia straightens her shoulders. And that's when I realize which Bershovs she means—the famous Russian circus family. This girl's great-grandparents were international circus stars.

We have sandwiches and salad in the cafeteria. Lights are out in the dorms at ten, but I'm still on West Coast time. Somehow I manage to sleep. In the morning there's a buffet breakfast in the cafeteria. Fresh fruit, all kinds of cheese, yogurt, bran muffins and the most delicious, most buttery croissants I've ever tasted.

"Welcome to circus camp!" Suzanne claps to get our attention. She explains that she wants us to feel at home but also wants us to understand that there are rules—and if we don't follow them, we'll be sent home. "No girls in the boys' dorm. No boys in the girls' dorm. No smoking, no drugs, no alcohol. No unsupervised practicing that could be considered dangerous in any of the training areas, or anywhere else for that matter, inside or outside the school. If there are any accidents, the camp could be sued. Shoes," she adds as an afterthought. "No bare feet in this building. Except in the shower."

Suzanne says we'll spend our first day getting to know each other. We're meeting up in la palestre in half an hour.

We're early, so Genevieve and I take our time getting to la palestre. "You smell like cookies," I tell her.

Genevieve does her hair-flip thing. "Thanks," she says. "It's my vanilla cologne. I guess you don't wear perfume?"

"I'm not into smelling like cookies."

"I'm not into smelling like sweat," Genevieve says with a smile.

"I don't smell like sweat," I tell her.

"What are you getting so worked up about? I never said you did."

On our way to la palestre, we spot two guys in one of the smaller, glassed-in studios. Both are short with dirty-blond hair. One is dressed in clothes that are way too big: a loose-fitting shirt and pants that look dangerously close to falling off. The other's clothes are way too small: a tight-fitting tank top and pants that stop six inches from the ground. The guys have their arms around each other's shoulders and are performing for a silver-haired gentleman sitting in a folding chair at the front of the studio.

We peer through the glass to see what they're doing. The guy in the too-big clothes must feel us watching, because he spins around to look at us. Genevieve and I both giggle when we see his red clown nose.

Genevieve nudges me. "Check out the old guy. It's Hugo Lebrun. From Cirque de la Lune."

"Oh my god, you're right."

One thing Genevieve and I have in common, besides climbing, is an obsession with Cirque de la Lune. My mom and I have been to eight Cirque de la Lune shows, mostly in Vancouver, and once when she took me to Las Vegas for my birthday.

Genevieve's never seen the Cirque live, but she's watched all its DVDs—and memorized every aerial act.

I can't believe I didn't recognize Hugo Lebrun. He's been in some of Cirque de la Lune's biggest productions. We're standing just a few feet away from the most famous clown on earth.

Both boys are looking at us now. The one dressed in baggy clothes is much better-looking than the one in the too-tight clothes—he has clear blue eyes and hair that curls at the nape of his neck. The other one's face is chubby and pockmarked.

The handsome one slides his hand down his side, reaches into his pocket and pretends to take out a cell phone. Now he points to the window where we're standing, then at the imaginary phone. He flips the phone open and begins tapping one fingertip on an invisible keypad. He glances back at the window, lifting one eyebrow as he holds the phone to his ear.

He's pretending to call me. Or Genevieve.

I hope it's me.

We both crack up. Hugo Lebrun laughs too.

Genevieve and I wave to the boys and to Hugo and head back down the hallway. Genevieve tucks her arm through mine. "I totally love circus camp," she says.

Even if we end up competing for the same spot, even if we disagree when it comes to makeup and perfume, it feels good to have a friend.

Genevieve leans in toward me. "You know that cute clown?" she says. "He's mine."

And because I don't know what to say to that, I don't say anything.

Three

All twenty-five of us are sitting in a circle on the floor of la palestre. A stranger who walked in now would know we're acrobats.

Rather than sitting on their heels or with one leg crossed over the other the way regular kids sit, Genevieve and Anastasia are doing the splits, their hands casually resting on their thighs. The handsome clown has one leg bent in front of him, the other stretched out behind him, and is holding his back toes with one hand. His partner has planted his palms by his sides and is supporting his weight on his arms.

They aren't performing—it's just how they sit.

Watching them confirms that circus camp is the right place for me. All my life, and especially before I got into gymnastics in grade three, I've felt different from other kids. None of them liked climbing stuff the way I did. Even back in kindergarten, I was the only one who slept with my feet propped up against the wall at naptime.

Suzanne leads the orientation. She wants us to say our names, where we're from and what our circus specialty is. The handsome clown is named Leo; his sidekick is Guillaume. They are from Belgium and have been training together as a pair for two years.

The first exercise, Suzanne explains, will help us get comfortable with each other. "I'll call out a body part—for example, elbow—and you're going to touch nine people's elbows. Got that?" She looks around the group. "Elbow!"

I feel bad for Hana, who doesn't seem to know what *elbow* means. I tap her elbow.

"Ahh." She nods. "*Pal-kkum-chi.*"

Soon all of us are racing around the room, tapping elbows and getting tapped. Leo winks when his fingers graze my elbow. Did he wink at Genevieve too?

"Knee!" Suzanne calls out, then "Ankle!"

When I tap Cécile's ankle, I notice her calves are rock hard. It must come from doing the tightrope.

I may not have learned everyone's name yet, but after a few rounds of this exercise, I've touched everyone in the room. Suzanne was right—it's a good way of getting comfortable with each other. Especially for people like us, who communicate better with our bodies than with words.

There's a trapeze in la palestre, a tightrope, and tissu and ropes for climbing. In a large open closet, I spot rows and rows of colorful juggling pins. Suzanne has explained that although we'll each be spending two hours every day working on our specialty, we'll have a chance to learn the other specialties too. I've tried juggling before, but I've never managed to get the hang of it.

Through the huge floor-to-ceiling window at one end of the room, I see a tall lopsided maple tree outside. The tree is so close to the terrace it provides a shady corner. I can just make out a furry brown squirrel zipping up the tree trunk, then leaping onto one of the branches. The branch is so light the squirrel's weight makes it rock. Another squirrel is dashing up the tree trunk now. This one stops short of the branch, as if he's worried he's not agile enough to make the leap his friend did. *You can do it, little squirrel,* I tell him in my head. *Don't let fear stop you.*

"Have any of you ever heard the expression 'All work and no play makes Jack a dull boy'?" Suzanne asks. None of us have, so Suzanne explains that it's not healthy for people to work, work, work all the time. They need to play too. "What makes circus so wonderful," Suzanne says, "is that your work is play. But you still need to work on it. That might sound confusing, but it's what circus is all about—a magic mix of work and play."

I nod when Suzanne says that. It's exactly why I love circus. I've just never heard anyone put the feeling into words before.

Guillaume points one finger at the middle of Leo's forehead. Leo falls backward to the floor, his tongue hanging out of his mouth like a dog's. Everyone laughs.

Suzanne checks her watch. "You have half an hour to play," she tells us. "Or work. Or both. Instructors will be on hand to supervise you."

Because the rope is there, I climb it. Anastasia, Genevieve, Leo and Guillaume watch as I grab the rope, wrap one foot around the bottom, then block it with my other foot. I need to be careful not to chafe the skin between my big toe and the one next to it. But I can't worry about that now. Besides, what's a little pain if you want to be a circus performer?

Up I go. First hands, then feet. Hands, then feet. My palms are burning, but I keep hoisting myself up, up, up. Then up some more. The ceiling must be thirty feet high in la palestre, a good ten feet higher than at the gym where I train in North Vancouver, but I'm not nervous. Just happy and excited. I'm nothing like that squirrel I saw outside. In no time, I'm at the top. Oh, it feels good to be up here!

"Beautiful!" Leo calls out, and I hope he doesn't mean just my climbing.

"My turn," Genevieve says when I've slid down the rope and am back on the giant round safety mat. The tissu are red and yellow and green, and I have to admit they make Genevieve look elegant as she begins to climb. She knows it, too, because she pauses halfway up, letting her long, perfectly blow-dried hair fall behind her like a black fan.

Leo and Guillaume lean back to watch her.

Climbing tissu is so much more common than climbing a rope. I'm glad I do the less common thing. That's the kind of circus performer I dream of being. An innovator, someone who works on the edge of what's new. Not just a girl like Genevieve who does what so many female circus performers already do.

As she climbs, Genevieve wraps her feet in the tissu. Now she throws herself backward into space and hangs just from her feet. It's a daring move. She lets her arms dangle, making her look like a human pendulum. Then she bends one knee, hooking it over the tissu. The second knee follows. She's showing us her frog move.

Leo puts two fingers in his mouth and whistles. Guillaume makes *ribbit*ing sounds.

When I look up, I see Genevieve grinning down at me. When she opens her mouth to laugh, I know what she's thinking. *I'll bet you can't do this, can you?*

Four

"See that guy?" Genevieve lifts her eyes toward a man in chef's whites standing near the long buffet table set up on the terrace. "You know what I heard? He's Etienne Montpellier's personal chef! Can you imagine being so rich you can hire your own chef?"

Etienne Montpellier owns Cirque de la Lune. He started out as a street performer and built the company into the world's most successful circus. The guy is worth gazillions.

Leo licks his lips. "No wonder these hamburgers are so good," he says.

Smoke billows out of two barbecues. At one of them, a chef is grilling regular hamburgers and hot dogs. At the other, another chef is grilling red-bean burgers and tofu hot dogs. From what I can tell, vegetarians outnumber carnivores two to one at circus camp.

Genevieve, Hana, Anastasia and I are sitting at a picnic table across from Leo and Guillaume.

Guillaume keeps sliding closer to Leo. Every time Guillaume does that, Leo rolls his eyes, swats Guillaume with the back of his hand and moves away. We all laugh when Leo comes close to falling off the bench. Guillaume tugs on Leo's arm, then makes a reeling motion as he pulls him back up.

"Do you two ever stop joking around?" Genevieve asks.

"Not if we can help it," they say at the exact same time, which makes us laugh some more.

"What is that you are eating?" Hana asks me. All she has on her plate is a tofu hot dog—and she's only taken the teensiest bite.

"It's quinoa salad."

Hana has never heard of quinoa. Apparently they don't serve it in Korea. "It's a grain. This salad has raisins and apricots in it too," I tell her.

She nods as if I have said something very deep.

The two chefs wheel their barbecues to the back of the terrace and move the buffet table out of the way. A rigger lays down safety mats. When the music starts, it's so low that at first I think I'm imagining it.

But it gets louder, and I realize it's that old Alice Cooper song "School's Out." Like me, Hana is tapping her foot. She may not have heard of quinoa, but she knows this song. I think about how there are so many people in this world and how music brings us closer. Circus does that too.

The lights on the terrace dim, then go out. When they come on again two minutes later, we see that two rows of old-fashioned wooden school desks have been set up on the mats. There's one long desk in front of the others. The spotlights shine down on a woman sitting behind the desk. She's wearing a black dress with a high collar and thick glasses with black rims. It takes me a minute to realize it's Suzanne.

"No more pencils! No more books!" Alice Cooper's voice wails through the speakers.

When he lands on the word *books*, Suzanne picks up two textbooks from a pile on her desk. She tosses one high into the air, and then, before it has time to land, she tosses up the other. I've seen people juggle balls and pins, but never books.

When we applaud, Suzanne picks up two more books and juggles those too.

I'm so focused on Suzanne, I hardly notice the other performers. Four of them have lined up single file. Each wears a black cape and a mortarboard with gold tassels.

"Look! There's Hugo Lebrun!" Leo points at the last performer.

When Hugo hears his name, he turns to our table and takes a deep bow. Leo and Guillaume stand up and bow back. Everyone laughs. Genevieve has a throaty laugh; Hana's giggle sounds like wind chimes.

I catch Leo winking at us as he sits back down.

The rigger pushes the desks together so they form a long flat surface. A performer jumps up onto the desks and does a triple somersault across them.

A second performer pedals backward across the stage on a unicycle.

"That's really hard to do," I hear someone at another picnic table whisper.

The guy on the unicycle hoists himself up so that he is balancing on the handlebars, and somehow—don't ask me how—he uses his weight to make the unicycle go backward. The crowd breaks into a round of noisy applause.

Suzanne is behind her desk, her hands on her hips, watching the others. She scowls when Alice Cooper sings the line *"No more teachers' dirty looks."*

On cue, the other performers whip off their capes and throw them down onto the mats. They are wearing gold lamé unitards that glitter under the spotlights. Why didn't I notice the tightwire before—or that the riggers have pulled out scaffolding from the side of the building? It must mean there's going to be an aerialist.

Two of the performers lift another performer up to the wire, and she takes tiny measured steps as she crosses its length. She steps halfway back, then does the splits along the wire. The crowd makes an approving *ooh.*

The rope climber is next. I get shivers as I watch him hoist himself up, working his arms, chest and legs. When he gets to the top, he flips upside down. All that's keeping him hanging is the knot he's tied over one foot. I look at the people sitting at my picnic table and at the tables near ours. I wonder if they are all thinking the same thing as me: *Will I ever be that good?*

Still hanging upside down, the rope climber releases a net basket. Inside it are hundreds of white paper airplanes. They flutter to the ground, and the show is over. We laugh, we applaud, and then we join in, singing and stomping our feet along with Alice Cooper. School is definitely out for the summer.

* * *

That night when I close my eyes in my top bunk, I still see images from the evening's performance.

Not long after that, I hear whimpering. I wonder if somehow a small dog has gotten into the dormitory. But then I realize someone in a lower bunk is crying—and trying to muffle the sound. It's hard to know what to do. Wait for the crying to end? Try to figure out who it is and whether there is something I can do to help?

The whimpering stops, then starts again.

Though I don't know for sure, it could be coming from the bunk right under mine, where Hana is.

I hear someone get out of one of the lower bunks and then the sound of slippers padding along the floor. More sniffling.

I need to pee, so I get up too.

Hana is slumped in the hallway, her hands over her face. Is that a tattoo of a rose on her lower back?

"Hana," I whisper, "can I help you?"

She shakes her head, so I leave to use the bathroom. When I come out, Genevieve is crouched on the floor beside Hana. "Poor thing is homesick," she says.

Hana's eyes are red from crying.

"Maybe you'll feel a little better tomorrow," Genevieve says.

"Would it help if you phoned your family in Seoul?" I ask.

Genevieve shoots me a look. "It's probably too expensive for Hana to phone Seoul."

"It isn't the money." Hana wipes her nose, then looks at Genevieve and me. "My parents are traditional Korean, meaning very strict. They did not like for me to come to North America. I do not want them to know I am so lonely for them."

Her face is solemn. "Please don't say to anyone I'm sick for home."

Genevieve and I promise not to tell.

"Cool tattoo. I guess you like roses," I say, hoping to distract Hana from her troubles.

Hana's dark eyes light up. "It is not a rose. It is *mugunghwa.* Korea's national flower."

Genevieve wants to see the tattoo. "I think we call that a hibiscus. Your parents can't be that strict if they let you get a tattoo."

When Hana shakes her head, I realize that mentioning the tattoo was a bad idea. "My parents know nothing about my tattoo," she whispers. "They would not have given permit."

It doesn't seem like a good moment to tell Hana we say *homesick*, not *sick for home*, and that parents give *permission*, not *permit.*

Five

Terence, our aerial coach, has sandy-blond hair he wears in a long ponytail down his back. That was him on the rope last night, dangling from one foot during the staff show.

When we walk into the area of la palestre where the tissu and climbing ropes are, Terence is sitting on a black vinyl cube. "We'll spend the morning reviewing basic climbs and descents," he says after we have introduced ourselves.

He begins by demonstrating a basic climb. "Base foot square," he says, looking down at his foot. "Base leg slightly forward. See how I'm using the ball of my upper foot to push the rope against my base foot, and how I'm pulling my shoulders down and opening my chest as I climb?"

"What does he think this is—kindergym?" Genevieve whispers to me.

Terence is up near the ceiling in no time. "If you climb a rope right," he calls down to us, "you'll never do a single chin-up. Because you'll never pull with just your arms. You step up the rope with the help of your arms and legs."

Genevieve nudges me. "Does he really think we haven't figured that one out yet?"

Later, Terence watches carefully as each of us demonstrates a climb.

"Flatten your foot a little more when you stomp down on the rope," Terence tells me. "That'll create more friction and give your arms a break."

He doesn't say a thing when Genevieve climbs the tissu. Just nods. He nods again when she slides down the tissu, making big circles with one arm at a time. That girl sure likes to show off.

We get four fifteen-minute breaks during the day. Some of the kids hang out on the mats. They stretch or chat or stare into space. Others go to the cafeteria for a snack—carrot sticks, bran muffins, herbal tea. Besides our three meals, we can get snacks at the cafeteria until five o'clock every day.

I'm thinking of grabbing a muffin, but Genevieve offers to show me how to do the frog move she demonstrated yesterday. I don't know if it's because she really wants to be helpful or because she wants to make sure I know she's a better climber than I'll ever be.

But I really want to learn that move.

Genevieve demonstrates. She starts with her back pressed flat on the mat. "You hook one leg over you, like this," she says. "Then you take the tissu—or in your case, the rope—with your opposite hand and grab the loose rope underneath with your free hand. Hold the rope tight with your knee, then wrap it once over your free leg and let go with both hands. It's easier than it looks." She gets up from the mat. "Your turn," she says.

Is it my imagination, or is there something snooty about her tone every time she says *rope*? "It sounds like you have something against rope," I say.

"There's nothing wrong with rope. I just happen to prefer tissu. It's more..." She pauses, as if she's searching for the right word. "Feminine."

"You mean old-fashioned," I say.

Genevieve sighs. "I mean feminine."

I know it's an insult—she's saying I'm not feminine enough because I don't wear eyeliner and blow-dry my hair. I won't let her get away with that. "There are more important things than what a person looks like."

"Yeah," Genevieve says, "that's true. Things like making a living. Maybe you haven't had to think about it, but there are more work opportunities for female aerialists who do tissu." She flips her hair back. "There are also more work opportunities for female aerialists who put some effort into their appearance."

"I'd rather put effort into my climbing," I tell her.

"Well, go ahead then," Genevieve says. "Show me your frog on the mat."

Genevieve watches closely while I try out the move. "Bend your legs when you let go with your hands. That's better. You've almost got it. Almost."

After lunch, we work on our non-specialties. Mine's juggling. So, it turns out, is Genevieve's.

I am surprised when Suzanne walks into the small gym and announces that she's our juggling coach. But I shouldn't be—not after we saw her juggle those textbooks at the staff show.

Suzanne drags a crate of colorful squishy balls to the front of the gym. "No, no, no," she says when Leo and Guillaume each grab three balls. "We start with one ball."

"One ball? You're kidding, right?" Leo exclaims.

"One ball," Suzanne says, and I remember how she scowled during her performance. I'm starting to think Suzanne is tougher than she looks.

We spend the first ten minutes on our backs, tossing a squishy ball up into the air and catching it—or in my case, occasionally catching it. "Lying down like this means you don't have to worry about your balance—and it's easier on your backbone," Suzanne tells us. Then, with our arms bent at the elbow, we lob the ball from one hand to the other. Even though the ball is soft and weighs practically nothing, I don't like the feeling of something flying into my face. Once, when Suzanne walks by the spot where I am practicing, she catches me closing my eyes when the ball is about to land. "Eyes open!" she says. "Never lose sight of the ball."

Before we move on to two squishy balls, Suzanne gets us to do some neck rolls. I'm glad, because although I don't want to be whiny, one side of my neck is already sore from tossing and catching one dumb ball.

"What comes next," Suzanne explains, "is all about rhythm. Wait for the first ball to reach the top of its arc." She gets down onto the mat to demonstrate. "When it does, you toss the second ball up into the air."

Only it isn't so easy to know when the first ball has reached the top of its arc, and now I have two flying objects to deal with. I fight the urge to shut my eyes.

I hear Genevieve laugh. When I turn to look at her, she is juggling her two balls in a way that looks effortless. Why does Genevieve have to be so darned good at everything?

Six

"Has your family really been in the circus for *ten* generations?" I ask Anastasia.

Four of us—Genevieve, Hana, Anastasia and I—are having iced coffee in a nearby café. It's called Jarry 2, because it's on the ground floor of an old industrial building at the corner of Jarry Street and Second Avenue. It has red-brick walls and pine floors—and a refrigerated display case loaded with desserts, all made with mountains of whipped cream. We are sharing two chocolate éclairs, which Hana has sliced into perfect halves.

"That's right—ten generations." Anastasia sweeps her hand so dramatically through the air that I worry she'll hit one of the hanging plants. "But we don't call it being *in* the circus. We Bershovs *are* the circus!"

I am about to ask Anastasia what makes the Russian circus so special, but I don't have to.

"Our Russian circus is like no other. We have never mocked a person. We have never used fat ladies or little people to make our audiences laugh. Russian circus performers are agile and daring, yes, but so are North American and"—Anastasia's eyes land for a moment on Hana—"Asian circus performers. What sets us Russians apart is another skill: we know how to connect with an audience, how to build a relationship with every person in the stands."

Though Anastasia was born in Moscow, she was educated at a posh boarding school outside London. Her parents wanted her to have other options—they thought she might become a lawyer or a doctor—but Anastasia says circus runs in her blood. "What's the point in trying to fight destiny?" she asks me. "I did cartwheels over the stacks in the school library. Besides, I don't much care for reading."

Hana peers over the rim of her glass. "Tell us about Anatoly Bershov," she says. "Please."

Her famous family is Anastasia's favorite topic, and, like the people sitting in the stands during a circus performance, we are a captive audience. I can hardly believe I am sitting here with a descendant of Anatoly Bershov, the finest tumbler in circus history. He is credited with inventing the act in which seven acrobats form a human pyramid, with the top tumbler balancing upside down on the head of the one under him. The act is a circus classic.

Anastasia reaches for her iced coffee. "Anatoly Bershov was born into a noble Russian family. He lived in a castle with dozens of servants and beluga caviar for every meal. But he was different from his brothers and sisters. Even as a boy, Anatoly was capable of extraordinary feats." She looks at Genevieve and me. "He climbed the tallest poplar in all of Moscow. And he once vaulted across the Volga River. In 1792 a traveling circus came by caravan to Moscow. Anatoly and his family attended the performance. For once, Anatoly felt he belonged. He never went home."

"Do you really think that part about his never going home is true?" Genevieve asks. "Wouldn't he have at least wanted to pack a few things? Some rubles, for example? Or some rubies? Or maybe some of that caviar?"

Anastasia ignores the question. Her voice turns dreamy. "Catherine the Great fell madly in love with Anatoly. He was much younger than her, but she liked younger men. Her husband, Peter the Third, was younger than her too. Catherine and Anatoly couldn't marry, of course. In the end, he fell in love with another acrobat. They had a son, Vladimir."

Hana's mouth falls open. "Vladimir Bershov." The way she says it, the name sounds like a prayer. "I read a book about him. It was translated into Korean."

"I didn't bother with the biography," Anastasia says.

"I guess you're also related to Valentina Bershov," Genevieve says.

"My third cousin," Anastasia answers with another wave of her hand.

Valentina Bershov is a trapeze artist and one of Cirque de la Lune's most famous stars. "My mom and I saw her perform last year in Vancouver. With the Cirque." Now I sound like I'm the one praying.

"Wow," Genevieve adds. "Can you imagine her life? Being part of Cirque de la Lune! She must make a ton of money."

Anastasia groans. "To tell you the truth, I don't understand the North American obsession with Cirque de la Lune. Yes, it's big and the performers are paid a lot. But there's more to life than money. There are hundreds of other circus troupes around the world, and some are more innovative than Cirque de la Lune. I've heard there's an excellent troupe right here in Montreal called Cirque Viva."

Genevieve crosses her arms over her chest. "Some of us need to worry about money. We're not all from famous families." She looks at me. "And we didn't all grow up in fancy houses with giant trees in our backyards. My father isn't some wealthy engineer. He drives a truck, and my mother does filing in an office. They've had to scrape together every nickel to pay for me to learn tissu. I want to pay them back one day."

I feel tension in the air after Genevieve says all that, but it disappears when Hana looks at Genevieve and says, "That is most honorable of you."

The waiter hands Anastasia the bill. "How much do we each owe you?" I ask, reaching for my wallet.

"Uh," Anastasia mumbles, "let me see..." Her brow furrows as she looks at the bill.

Genevieve grabs the bill from Anastasia. "With the tip, it comes to $4.50 each."

If I hadn't been sitting so close to Anastasia, I might not have heard her sigh. Why is she relieved Genevieve took the bill? What was it Anastasia said about not caring for reading? She may be a Bershov, and she may have gone to a British boarding school, but Anastasia's life isn't any more perfect than any of ours. Not if she has trouble reading.

"Why are you looking at me funny?" Anastasia asks.

"I'm not looking at you," I lie.

Soon, thank goodness, we are talking about other things. Hana wants to know whether there were Bershovs who died during circus performances. It's a grisly thought, but we're all curious to know the answer.

Anastasia looks down at the pine floor. "Ivan Bershov broke his back when he fell from the top of a human pyramid. Natalya Bershov was mauled to death by a lion."

Genevieve makes a gulping sound.

"Tragic, yes," Anastasia says. "But as we all know, danger is part of circus life. If regular people could do what we do—form human pyramids, fly on the trapeze—and if there were no chance of things going terribly wrong, the stands would be empty."

Anastasia is right. That danger she's talking about? It's one of the reasons I'm hooked on circus.

Seven

Tuesday after breakfast, we have flex training in one of the small studios downstairs. Gillian, our flexibility coach, has arranged the mats on the floor. She isn't one for small talk. "Let's get down to work!" she calls out as we file into the room. "On your mats! Let's go! Now!"

Gillian looks strong. She's short and muscular, which makes me think she was probably a circus tumbler.

Unless, of course, she was an army sergeant. Because that's how Gillian runs flex class—like it's boot camp and we're soldiers in her private army.

"Start by loosening up your wrists and ankles," she commands. We press our wrists down on the mats, then shake out our hands. Next, we stretch our ankles, then shake those out too.

Gillian barks out one instruction after another. "We'll begin with the pike stretch. Sitting up tall, legs stretched out in front of you, toes pointed. Now keep your backs long and reach for those toes! Or better still, past them! Let's go!" She counts off the seconds. "One, two, three...get deeper into that stretch...five, six...deeper still!"

The stretch is making my hamstrings sore, but it's a good sore—and it's waking me up. I reach for my toes and then a little farther.

"Eight, nine, nine and a half, nine and three-quarters"—Gillian is trying to be funny by counting halves and quarters, but we're working too hard to laugh—"ten!"

Hana is on the next mat. I heard her sobbing again last night. At breakfast, I asked whether she had phoned her parents. She shook her head. "I sent a text message saying I am well. If we speak by telephone, I am afraid I will become weak and want to go home. I must try to be more strong—for my parents and for me."

Six more pike stretches in a row and soon my muscles aren't just warm—they're on fire.

Gillian circulates around the room. She shakes her head when she sees Cécile's toes, which are not pointed. "In gymnastics class, you probably learned to do this exercise with flexed toes. But you're training for the circus now, and I said *point your toes.* Pointed toes look prettier than flexed toes. Details like that matter in circus. Seven, eight, nine..."

Genevieve, who is in the row in front of me, turns in my direction and smiles when Gillian says the word *prettier.* I know what she's thinking: *I told you so.*

Gillian only gives us thirty-second breaks between exercises. It's a good thing I filled my water bottle before class. I take a quick swig. Water dribbles down my chin and onto my chest, but there's no time to wipe it off. Gillian is making us do another pike stretch.

After the pike stretches are done, Gillian explains why flex training is so important. "In this room, you won't only be developing flexibility, but also strength and endurance."

I think of what Hana said about trying to be stronger.

"As circus performers," Gillian continues, "you'll need all three of those skills. And, of course, the more flexible you are, the less the chances are that you'll injure yourselves."

Though only a few of the students in flex class are specializing in contortion, Gillian wants us to do some pretty advanced moves, starting with the bridge. She makes us lie on our bellies and then use our hands to push ourselves up from the mats and move into downward dog position. "Now bend your left knee and bring your left foot to your left shoulder. Grasp your foot with your hand," Gillian says. "One, two..."

I feel Hana watching me, trying to figure out what Gillian wants us to do. I wish I could tell Gillian that Hana probably doesn't know what the word *grasp* means, but I don't want to embarrass her.

Gillian makes us go from the bridge into a position she calls the pretzel. "Without moving your legs, bend your arms and drop your chest to the floor. Eyes ahead of you! That's right! Now you've got it!"

After those killer chest and back bends, we move into the splits. Gillian gets us to fold our mats up like accordions. Then we rest one heel on the mat so that the foot is about eight inches off the floor. My thigh muscles are throbbing.

"Breathe into the stretch," Gillian tells us.

I inhale deeply and take an even longer time to exhale. The memory of how the tightwire performer did full splits on her wire the other night pushes me to go a little deeper.

When I look at Hana, I see that her thigh is pressed flat against the mat, her face perfectly calm. Leo and Guillaume are at the back of the gym, but I can hear their raspy breathing.

When Gillian comes to where I am, she pauses to watch me, then presses down on my hips and lower back. She's telling me to go farther into the stretch.

When I look into the mirror at the front of the room, my eyes meet Genevieve's, and I see she is grimacing. "It might be easier if you bring your foot in a little closer," Gillian is telling her. Genevieve sighs.

I may not be as flexible as Hana, but at least Gillian didn't tell me to bring my foot in closer. Wanting to be better than Genevieve makes me push myself even harder. I want to show her that pretty only goes so far, that what really counts in circus is skill—and effort. I'm working my thigh muscles so hard now they won't stop shaking, even when I release the stretch a bit.

It's as if Gillian can read my thoughts. "The only one you should be comparing yourself to is yourself. Every body is different," she says from the back of the gym. "Flexibility training is not a competition. Circus camp is about improving your skills and having fun. It's *not* a contest."

But we all know that isn't true. There is not much chance that Genevieve and I will both be picked for MCC. I need to be better than her in every way. And the truth is, I don't know if I can be.

I press down harder. My whole body feels jangly, like I've gone too long without eating.

"Breathe deeply!" Gillian calls out.

I'm pushing so hard my breaths have become shallow, and they're coming too quickly.

I don't even notice that I'm crying. It's Hana who does. She comes out of her stretch and leans toward me. "Oh, Mandy," she says, reaching out her hand to wipe the tears from my cheeks. "Is something wrong?"

Gillian gives us a water break, and I head for the girls' bathroom. I'm refilling my water bottle when Genevieve and Anastasia push open the bathroom door. The two of them are laughing. "Can you believe that girl?" Genevieve is saying. She brings her fingers to her forehead and makes the letter *L*. "What a capital-*L* loser!"

I cringe, because they must mean me. Did they notice that I was crying?

"Imagine being fifteen years old and crying for Mummy and Daddy. Next thing you know she'll be wetting her bed!" Anastasia says.

My first reaction is relief that I'm not the capital-*L* loser Genevieve and Anastasia are laughing about.

My second reaction is that Genevieve and I both promised Hana we would not tell anyone she was homesick, and Genevieve has broken her promise.

Genevieve is probably not the best person to get into a fight with. But what she's done isn't right—and Hana has no one else to defend her.

Genevieve purses her lips and flips her dark hair in front of the mirror. Because I'm still standing at the sink, I speak to her reflection.

It feels easier than speaking directly to her. "I thought you promised you wouldn't say anything about Hana."

Anastasia nudges me with her elbow. "Don't be a sourpuss," she says. "Genevieve was only telling me a funny story. Don't you like funny stories?"

This time I don't say what I'm thinking: laughing at someone else's troubles isn't my idea of funny.

Eight

For many of us, coming to circus camp is our first time in Montreal. So the directors want us to get a chance to experience the city. Thursday afternoon, camp ends at two thirty. A red double-decker bus, the kind you'd expect to see in London, picks us up in front of the college. We're taking a private tour, with a stop in Old Montreal before the bus returns us to our dorms.

Suzanne and Hugo will be our chaperones. They sit at the back of the bus on the first floor, where it is air-conditioned. The rest of us race to the top deck, which has no roof. It's hot and humid, but after spending most of the week indoors at circus camp, the heat and humidity feel good on my skin.

I sit with Hana, who is wearing a wide-brimmed straw hat. Even though the bus isn't moving, she is already snapping photographs with the smallest camera I have ever seen. Leo and Guillaume are sitting in front of us. When the engine starts and the tour guide's voice comes crackling through the speakers, Leo turns and grins. I feel myself blush.

Guillaume drapes his arm around Leo's shoulder and makes a show of pulling him close. "Will you stop flirting with the girls and pay a little attention to *moi* instead?" Guillaume says loudly. "Have you forgotten that I am your circus partner?"

"Those two are so funny," Hana says to me. "I think the handsome one likes you."

"He's just teasing," I tell Hana, but I hope she's right.

The tour guide is giving us general information about the city. Montreal is an island. It's the second-largest city in Canada, with a population of over one and a half million. French is the official language. Montreal is named for Mount Royal, the mountain in the city's center. We'll be driving through Mount Royal Park at the end of our tour.

There's a lot of traffic on the Metropolitan Highway. When the bus comes to a halt, Leo and Guillaume wave at people in their cars. "Let's see if we can make them laugh," Guillaume says to Leo.

The two boys juggle invisible balls and pretend to duel and play the violin. Hana and I keep count of how many drivers laugh. Soon we are up to seventeen. It's a good way for Hana to practice counting in English.

About twenty minutes later, the tour bus is winding its way through the city center. Sherbrooke Street is a wide boulevard where the Museum of Fine Arts is located. A narrower side street leads us down to Ste-Catherine Street, where all the shops are.

Genevieve peers over the side of the bus. "The girls in Montreal all look so stylish. I wish the bus would slow down so we could get a better look at the store windows."

But when the light turns green, the bus picks up speed. Genevieve shakes her head wistfully.

"To your right is 1000 de la Gauchetière. At 205 meters—or 673 feet—it is the tallest building in Montreal," the tour guide says. "There's a skating rink inside that is open year-round. If you didn't bring your skates, it is possible to rent a pair."

Genevieve and Anastasia are sitting across the aisle from Leo and Guillaume. Leo leans over toward Genevieve. "How would you like to go skating with me sometime?" he asks her.

I can't help feeling a little jealous that he didn't ask me.

Genevieve squeals. "I'd love to go skating with you!" She says it so loudly the whole bus can hear her.

"I'll be there too!" Guillaume chimes in. "Leo and I travel as a pair."

The next attraction is the Notre-Dame Basilica in Old Montreal. "This church is one of the best examples in North America of Gothic Revival architecture. Notice the ornate towers at both ends," the guide says. "Our next stop is the Old Port. There, you'll have ninety minutes to explore the old city by yourselves. We meet back at the bus at six o'clock sharp."

From the bus, Guillaume and Leo have spotted an ice-cream shop called La Crémière. They want to go there first. The rest of us follow.

De la Commune Street, which overlooks the port, is full of tourists. Hana has never tasted maple, and she wants to try the maple ice cream.

I see Genevieve elbowing her way through the crowd, trying to get closer to Leo.

"Do you like maple?" Hana asks me.

"Sure I like it. I'm Canadian, aren't I?"

"What does maple taste like?"

"It's hard to describe. A bit like honey. But more buttery."

"Do you mean butterscotch?" I can tell from the way she says it that Hana is proud to know the word *butterscotch*.

"You'll have to try it and see for yourself."

We sit on the benches outside La Crémière to eat our ice cream. Hana's forehead is scrunched in a way that makes me think she can't decide whether she likes maple. I'm having strawberry.

Someone tugs on my hand. I can't help grinning when I see it's Leo. He gestures for me to follow him.

"I won't be long," I whisper to Hana.

"Let's go have some fun," Leo says.

So Hana was right. Leo *does* like me. So what if he invited Genevieve to go skating? Leo grabs my hand and whisks me down one of the cobblestone streets. It feels like we're dancing.

Leo and Guillaume have visited Montreal before, so Leo knows his way around the old city. He wants to take me to Place Jacques-Cartier. He says it's just around the corner.

When we get there, I understand why he's brought me. The square is not only beautiful—lined with bars and cafés, customers sitting outside at round tables, colorful petunias in the flower boxes—but is also full of street performers. A man in a billowy yellow clown costume walks on stilts. Another man juggles pins, and two girls play fiddle. I think about Etienne Montpellier and how he started out as a street performer.

Leo leads me to where the juggler is performing. This guy makes juggling four pins look easy. When he misses a catch and one pin clatters to the ground, Leo picks it up.

Leo holds the pin to his chest as if it's a baby. "Wah!" he cries out, the way a baby would. Then he jumps as if the sound has startled him.

The crowd laughs.

"Wah!" Leo cries again. He rocks the pin back and forth in his arms, and the crowd laughs even harder. The juggler laughs so hard he has to hold on to his belly. He doesn't seem to mind that Leo is stealing the show.

Leo tosses the pin into the air, and the juggler catches it.

We are listening to the fiddlers' performance when Leo's cell phone rings. I can hear Guillaume's voice on the other end. "Where are you? It's almost six."

"You're so lovely," Leo says to me, "I lost track of the time." Then he dances me back to the double-decker bus. I wonder if all the others can tell what fun the two of us have had.

* * *

Later, when we are back in the dorm and brushing our teeth in the girls' bathroom, I think about how to break the news to Genevieve that Leo likes me. It will be hard for her because I know she likes him too. Still, I decide it's better to be honest.

"Genevieve..." I begin.

But she has something to tell me first. "Oh, Mandy," she says, grabbing my hand. "Guess what?

Leo and I are going skating on Sunday! He didn't use the word *date*, but I know that's what he meant. I'm going to have to get up super early on Sunday to straighten my hair."

Nine

Why would Leo dance in the street with me in the afternoon *and* ask Genevieve on a skating date? Can't he make up his mind which one of us he likes better? I want to tell Hana how it's bothering me, but I decide not to because her homesickness gets worse at bedtime.

I don't want to tell my mom either. She'll say I'm too young to be worrying about boys. But I'm in the mood to hear her voice, and it's been a few days since I phoned home. I grab my phone and go down the hallway to make the call. I'm afraid Hana will get even more homesick if she knows I'm speaking to my parents.

My dad answers. "Your mom's out. She's gone for a swim. It's awfully hot here."

"Here too."

I wait for him to ask how things are going at circus camp, but he doesn't. "I'm working on a big report," he says. "Why don't you phone back this time tomorrow?"

Those are my dad's words. But I know he's saying something else—he's still upset that I haven't given up my dream to make a life in the circus.

"You being careful?" he asks just before I hang up.

I hate how he is always worrying about me. It's like a sickness he can't control. "Can you try to quit worrying?" I ask.

"I can try," he says, "only I don't think it'll work."

* * *

The next day in aerial class, I have trouble concentrating. "Point your toes!" Terence has to remind me more than once when I'm climbing the rope. "I want to see you paying more attention to your form, Mandy!"

But when I work on keeping my toes pointed, I lose track of what my arms are doing.

"Reach higher!" Terence tells me. "Keep those shoulders away from your ears! Lengthen your neck! I want to see you channel some giraffe!"

Is it my imagination, or is he losing patience with me?

Terence must know something is wrong because when we're all sitting on the mats, he gives us a little lecture. "Circus is physical," he says. "But it's mental too. Circus performers need to be able to focus no matter what's going on in the rest of their lives. Without focus, the moves get sloppy. And without focus, there's a greater danger of injury. Sometimes even serious injury." Because Terence makes a point of *not* looking at me when he says this, I know his advice is meant for me.

So when it's my turn again, I will myself not to think about how it felt to dance in the streets of Old Montreal with Leo, or to remember that he has asked Genevieve to go skating on Sunday. Instead, I focus on my body and the rope.

This time, I use every muscle in my shoulders to hoist myself up, and my toes feel stiff from pointing them so hard. I know the friction from the rope is chafing the skin between my big toe and the one next to it, but I don't feel the pain. All I want to do is concentrate on my form.

"Better," Terence says.

I'm beginning to think the coaches at circus camp aren't big on compliments.

Terence is right. If I want to make it in circus, I'll need to train my mind as hard as I train my body.

Only just when I am thinking that, the side of the rope brushes against my cheek, and I'm suddenly remembering the feel of my dad kissing me goodnight when I was a little girl. *You being careful?* his voice asks in my head.

"You're losing your concentration again, Mandy!" Terence bellows from the mats. How can he tell?

Unlike me, Genevieve does not seem to be having any trouble concentrating. When it's her turn, Terence asks for only the tiniest adjustments. "Open your chest a little more. Give yourself to the audience."

At the end of climbing class, Terence gets us to do some forward bends on the mats. Genevieve and I face each other. "Oh my god," she says, staring at my feet. "What have you done to your toes? They're totally gross!"

I look down and see that the skin between my first two toes has begun to bleed. How could I not have noticed? I was so focused on trying to be focused that I didn't even feel it.

Terence says I should put on some antibiotic cream when I get upstairs. I wonder if bleeding toes counts as one of the injuries he was talking about before.

I have antibiotic cream in my cosmetics bag. I'm sitting on one of the lower bunks in our dorm, applying the cream, when Anastasia taps me on my shoulder.

"Use this instead." She hands me a tube of Krazy Glue.

"Are you joking?" I ask.

"Would I joke about a circus injury? Antibiotic cream is good for preventing infection. But with Krazy Glue, you'll be back on the rope tomorrow! It's an old Russian circus trick."

"You have Krazy Glue in Russia?" I ask, taking the tube from Anastasia and squirting a little of the liquid between my toes.

"Krazy Glue might be an American product, but I heard that a Russian man, a friend of my uncle Boris, invented it. He mixed together water and corn syrup. My uncle Boris was a famous equestrian..." Anastasia has launched into another one of her family stories.

It's a long story. But I listen to every word. It's the only way I can think of to show my gratitude.

Ten

Suzanne says there will be a special surprise for us tonight.

"Is it food?" Guillaume calls out. "Are we going to try Montreal's famous smoked meat?"

"Does it have something to do with Cirque de la Lune?" Genevieve asks.

"Of course not!" Suzanne looks away when she says that. Which is how we know for sure the surprise has something to do with Cirque de la Lune.

"Maybe the Cirque's team of talent scouts wants to meet us," Genevieve says after Suzanne has left the cafeteria. We are eating breakfast—homemade granola, Greek yogurt, poached eggs, whole-grain bread, bran muffins and fresh fruit.

I like eating healthy food, but there is so much of it at circus camp that I can't blame Guillaume for dreaming about smoked meat.

"Maybe the Cirque performers—and all of their understudies—have come down with the flu and Etienne Montpellier wants us to fly to Vegas to help him out," Guillaume says.

"I think you should put me in charge of negotiating with Etienne. We'll need suites at the Wynn Hotel and round-the-clock room service!" Leo adds.

"I have figured out the surprise!" Anastasia announces. She pauses. Even when she's just hanging out, Anastasia knows how to put on a show.

"What is it?" Genevieve and Hana ask.

"The Cirque de la Lune troupe must be developing a new show. They probably want to test it out on us."

"Do you mean we might get to see a Cirque de la Lune show before anyone else in all the world?" Genevieve asks.

Leo grins. "I want to say one thing. This camp is my idea of heaven. Even without the smoked meat."

* * *

Anastasia was right. Suzanne asked us to meet her at a quarter to six at the MCC entrance, and we arrive to find that our coaches are there too. This time there is no red double-decker bus waiting in front of the building. Instead, we cross Second Avenue and walk over to the Cirque de la Lune headquarters.

A young man and woman dressed like playing cards, their faces painted white, usher us into a small auditorium. On the way, we pass paintings and sculptures connected to circus. A bronze strongman carries a beautiful girl on his shoulders. In a painting in an ornate gold frame, a girl in a frilly dress dances on top of a white horse. "Chagall painted that one," Hana whispers.

I'd heard that Etienne Montpellier collects art, and I wish we had more time to admire his collection, but the ushers move us along. They make us stop at a small table where each of us has to sign a waiver. Even our coaches have to. What we see tonight must remain top secret. When I am signing, Leo brushes my elbow with his. "You look radiant this evening, Mata Hari," he says. I turn away and pretend not to have heard him.

The stage is set up to look like a giant tea party. There are half a dozen tables decorated with lace tablecloths. When a beautiful girl wearing a blue dress with a white apron steps onstage, I understand why the ushers are dressed like playing cards. We're about to see an *Alice in Wonderland* circus performance.

Alice's aerial hoop is as tall as she is, but she whips it forward, skipping through it so quickly that all we can see is a white glow. Alice is entering Wonderland. When the bottom of her dress expands so that Alice is towering over us, I try to figure out how they did it. Is there someone standing underneath her? Could there be two or even three people there?

There's no time to figure it out. Tweedledum and Tweedledee are doing a juggling routine. Only they're not juggling balls or pins, they're juggling toy mice. They each balance a mouse on the tip of their nose, then toss the mice over their heads. They spin around just in time to catch the mice with their toes and send them flying back up into the air.

There's a Mad Hatter too. He's a tightrope walker, and he crosses the rope carrying an oversized, flowered teapot. He keeps pretending he is about to fall—he makes the funniest faces when that happens—but, of course, he never does. Once, when he wobbles, he actually collapses, flattening his spine along the rope—and pours some tea into his mouth. Then he reaches into his pocket for a sugar packet, tears it open and swallows the sugar too. Leo and Guillaume squeal with laughter.

A Caterpillar tumbler blows smoke rings out of his nose as he cartwheels across the stage. He extends one arm, allowing Alice to step onto his hand, and then he raises her high into the air. His face drips with sweat, but his expression is blissed out.

The entire cast sits down for tea. The Red Queen arrives by trapeze, landing on top of a fluffy white cake.

When the show is over, the cast returns to take a bow. We're all clapping like crazy except for Anastasia, who is just tapping her palm with her fingertips. Maybe she thinks the performance could have been edgier and more innovative.

I notice now that Alice looks very Russian. She has pale-blond hair, pale skin and light blue eyes set wide apart. When it's time for her final bow, she positions herself to face Anastasia and takes a deep bow. It is, of course, her way of paying tribute to the Bershovs. If it were me, I'd feel embarrassed, but Anastasia nods graciously.

"Look," Genevieve says. We're on our way out, and she is eyeing a tall thin man at the back of the room, close to the other entrance to the auditorium. "It's him! Etienne Montpellier! He must have come in during the show!" She grabs my arm. "Let's go meet him."

"Genevieve, we can't. What would we say?"

Genevieve ignores my protests. She drags me down the corridor and back in through the other entrance. Except by then, Etienne Montpellier is gone. I don't know if I'm more relieved or disappointed.

Another man, dressed all in black, is standing where Etienne Montpellier was. He is making notes on his iPad.

"Do you know where Etienne Montpellier went?" Genevieve asks him.

The man looks up. "Excuse me?"

"We want to know where Mr. Montpellier went," Genevieve says.

"He had another engagement," the man says. When he looks down at his iPad, I know he wants to get back to whatever he was doing. But Genevieve won't let him.

"Who are you?" she asks him.

"Genevieve!" I whisper.

"My name is Reginald Dubuc."

"Do you work for Cirque de la Lune too?" Genevieve asks.

"You could say so." Reginald hesitates, as if he's deciding whether he should tell us more. "I handle admissions at the MCC."

"Oh my god," Genevieve says, and the man laughs. For once, Genevieve is too overwhelmed to speak.

I take a breath. "We're aerialists," I manage to say. "With the circus camp."

"Ahh," Reginald says.

Genevieve has gotten her voice back. "Does that mean you've heard of us?"

Reginald laughs again. "I have heard there are many talented young people at this summer's camp. So you say you two are aerialists?"

I turn slightly, then push back my shoulders so Reginald will notice my deltoids. "I do rope."

Genevieve flips back her hair. "I do tissu."

Reginald looks at me, then at Genevieve, then back at me. "Well then, I suppose I'll be seeing one of you at the MCC next year."

"One of us?" Genevieve asks.

"That's right," Reginald says. "I thought you already knew. We only have one spot available for an aerialist at the MCC next year."

I can't believe Genevieve hadn't already figured that one out.

Eleven

On Sunday morning, la palestre is open for anyone who feels like practicing. A couple of coaches are there to supervise. When we come in, they are huddled together on metal folding chairs, sipping coffee from reusable cups.

Genevieve, Anastasia, Hana and I head for the long blue spring floor designed for tumbling. We warm up with a few somersaults, but soon we're doing cartwheels and then roundoff back handsprings. The floor makes a *bam-bam* sound every time we land on it.

The spring floor is surrounded by large rectangular pits, each of them filled with oversized yellow Styrofoam cubes. If we miss our mark, the cubes will ensure a cushy landing.

The floor is wide enough for two girls to use at once. While I await my turn, I dive into one of the pits. Just for fun. Wading between the Styrofoam cubes makes me feel like a little kid again.

Next thing I know, Genevieve is diving in too. When I see her body flying toward me, I step away as quickly as I can. What is she trying to do—crash into me?

Genevieve is on her knees, grinning up at me. "Did I mention Leo is taking me skating today?" she asks.

"You mentioned it." I almost add that she's mentioned it a thousand times, but I don't want her to know I care.

"He really likes me."

"If you say so."

Genevieve wades closer to where I am, until her face is only inches away from mine. "Of course I say so. And you're wasting your time flirting with him."

I don't know what bothers me more—the fact that her face is so close to mine or that she's accusing *me* of flirting with Leo.

"I'm not a flirt," I say. "Besides, I can't help it if he likes me too."

"He doesn't!" Genevieve's voice carries in the air. One of the coaches tilts his head in our direction.

"He does too. But you know what, Genevieve? Some of us have more important things on our minds than boys."

"Like what?" she says.

"Like circus."

Genevieve makes a snorting sound. "If there's only room for one aerialist at the MCC, we both know who it'll be. Me! Not just because I'm a better climber than you are, but because I do tissu."

It's my turn to snort. "Tissu's a cliché. Rope is way more interesting."

Genevieve's eyes are shining. "Interesting? Interesting only goes so far! People come to the circus to see something—and someone—beautiful."

"They want more than beauty. They want innovation!" I don't mean to raise my voice, but Genevieve is getting to me.

"You're just mad you don't do tissu!" Genevieve hisses.

"That's the dumbest thing I ever heard!"

The coach stands up from his folding chair. But it's Hana who intervenes. She somersaults into the pit, landing next to me. In seconds, she bounces up on her feet, inserting herself between Genevieve and me.

"If you two keep fighting, you will make trouble for all of us!" Hana raises her eyes toward the coach, who is ambling to the pit.

"Everything okay over there, ladies?" the coach calls out.

"Everything's fine!" I call back.

Hana bows her head, then raises it to give a small smile to the coach.

He heads back to his chair, reassured by Hana's good manners. "Keep it that way," he hollers.

When the three of us have climbed out of the pit, Hana brings her backpack from where she left it at the side of the room. She unzips the pack and shows us the thermos inside. "It's *boricha*. Barley tea in English. I brought it with me from Korea. You two must try it. Right away. Boricha helps when you feel nervous."

"I'm not nervous." I want Genevieve to know I'm not afraid of her—that I'm not afraid of anything.

Hana says we must go straightaway to the cafeteria for cups. She invites Anastasia to come along too.

I walk with Hana, who is still babbling about boricha tea. Anastasia and Genevieve are up ahead, walking close together. Something Genevieve says makes Anastasia giggle.

Then Anastasia turns around to look at me. "You two were fighting over Leo?" Her eyes are laughing.

"Not just Leo," I mutter.

"Well, there's no use fighting over him," Anastasia says. "Everyone knows he and Guillaume are a couple. They've been going out since last summer."

"Really?" I say.

Genevieve puts her hands on her hips. "Are you joking?" she asks.

Anastasia gives us each a look that seems to say we will never—ever—be as sophisticated as a member of the Bershov family. "Would I joke about something like that?"

I can't believe I didn't figure out that Leo and Guillaume are together. And that I was convinced Leo liked me. The only thing that cheers me up is Genevieve not having figured it out either.

The four of us have to walk a long corridor before we reach the staircase that will take us down to the cafeteria. Along the way, we walk by the windows that look out over Second Avenue.

I notice a worker adjusting the Canadian flag hanging outside the Cirque de la Lune headquarters. "Look," I say. "The flag. What do you think's going on out there?"

Anastasia presses her face to the window. "Oh my god," she whispers. "They only fly a flag at half-mast when someone dies."

We hear the elevator doors slide open at the end of the hallway. Terence comes flying out toward us. For the first time, I notice the fine lines around his eyes.

"Why are they lowering the flag?" Anastasia asks him. "Who died?"

Terence wipes his nose. Has he been crying? "We just found out there was an accident earlier this morning at Cirque Viva," he tells us. "A climber died during practice." He pauses before he adds,

"It was someone I went to school with. Many years ago." He looks down the hallway. "In this building."

Anastasia slumps forward.

I bring my hand to my mouth.

Genevieve gasps.

Hana drops her thermos of tea. It tumbles out of her backpack and rolls down the corridor.

It isn't until later that I realize neither Genevieve nor I bothered asking whether the climber who died did tissu or rope.

Twelve

I don't want to be alone. Not after Terence's news. The other girls must feel the same way because when Hana suggests we go hang out in the MCC library, we are all quick to agree.

The library windows overlook the small gym, and from here we can see a student swinging back and forth on the trapeze. She's swinging so peacefully, I decide she must not yet have heard that a local circus performer is dead.

Dead.

I can't get the word out of my mind.

I've known circus performers who've been injured—who've sprained ribs or ankles, who've dislocated shoulders...I even knew a trampolinist who broke her arm—but never anyone who died. It's weird to think it could have happened while we were eating poached eggs in the cafeteria this morning.

Anastasia sits down at one of the computer terminals. Hana flips through a book about the history of circus. Genevieve and I seem to have made an awkward truce. We sit at opposite ends of the couch, watching a DVD of a performance by Circa, an Australian circus troupe that performed in Montreal last summer.

Genevieve fast-forwards the DVD to get to the climbing act. A redheaded woman with muscular shoulders climbs the tissu with the speed and ease of a monkey.

"Nice," Genevieve says to the screen.

"I wonder if the climber who died was doing tissu or rope," I say quietly.

Genevieve doesn't lift her eyes from the screen. "How should I know?" She sounds annoyed.

"Don't you care that a climber died?"

"I care. I just don't want to think about it right now," Genevieve says.

Maybe she's right. Maybe I shouldn't think about it either. I try to concentrate on the monkey woman's number instead. She is dangling from the red fabric by one ankle.

But then I start thinking about all the reasons why rope is better than tissu. A rope is rough and natural—there is nothing pretty about it. With rope, the focus stays on the performer. With tissu, the audience gets distracted by the beauty—the bright colors and the soft swish—of the Lycra.

Of course, I can't say any of this to Genevieve. We'd just get into another fight. From the way she has burrowed into her corner of the couch, her hands crossed over her chest, I decide she must be as upset as I am about the climber's death, even if she won't talk about it.

The librarian is hunched over Anastasia's computer. She's a tall woman who wears funky clothes, and today she has on a colorful artist's smock. She must know Anastasia has trouble reading, because she is pointing at the screen and explaining something to Anastasia. They both shake their heads and sigh. That's when I realize Anastasia is not checking her email. They are googling this morning's accident. Has it already made the news?

I pop up from the couch and head over to the computer. Genevieve stays on the couch, eyes glued to the screen, though I feel her gaze flutter and land on me when I get up.

The librarian moves over to make room for me. I was right. An article from the Montreal *Gazette* website is on the computer screen. The headline makes something catch in my throat. *Rope Climber Dies in Tragic Circus Accident.*

The librarian pats my elbow. Is it because she knows rope is my specialty at circus camp? I try to read the article, but the words keep getting blurry. An aerialist with Cirque Viva plummeted forty-five feet to her death earlier this morning. There will be an investigation, but preliminary reports indicate the aluminum carabiner to which the rope was attached broke. The victim was a woman, though her name has not yet been released. Several of the victim's fellow circus performers witnessed the accident.

I'm imagining what it would feel like to fall forty-five feet, to hear my friends' screams in the background. I close my eyes to make the picture—and the sounds—go away, but it doesn't help.

Leo picks that moment to burst into the library. Other people enter a room; they walk or, if they're in a hurry, they run. Leo bursts in.

He stops at the circulation desk. "Where's Genevieve?" His voice echoes in the room.

Genevieve doesn't look up from the screen. "She isn't here!" she calls back.

Leo doesn't get the message. He marches over to the couch. Now he notices me at Anastasia's computer. "Hey, girls," he says to all of us, "you coming skating or what?"

Genevieve keeps ignoring him.

When I look up at him, he walks over to the computer. "I guess you didn't hear about the accident," I whisper.

Leo freezes. "What accident?"

"An aerialist with Cirque Viva died this morning. They think the carabiner broke," I tell him.

"Oh no," Leo says.

Genevieve has finally stopped watching the DVD. She comes over to the computer. So does Hana.

We're all looking at the screen, not saying anything. Maybe because there are no words.

The librarian wipes her cheek.

That's when I realize that even if the *Gazette* website hasn't published the name of the aerialist who died, the librarian too may already know who the woman is. Didn't Terence tell us she was a student at MCC?

"Did you know her?" I ask the librarian.

"We all knew her." The librarian's voice is soft and sad. "Louise and Terence trained together. At one point, they competed for the same position..." Her voice trails off, as if she's remembering Louise and Terence together in la palestre.

"I guess we're not going skating," Leo says.

"We're not," Genevieve and I say at the same time.

So much for our catfight.

Thirteen

After the news of Louise's death, the mood at circus camp changes.

It's less noisy; everyone is more serious. But as Suzanne tells us on Monday morning, the show has to go on. She gestures to the flag outside—it will fly at half-mast all week. "Those of us who knew Louise will never forget her. But she'd want all of you to keep training, to keep doing your best, to keep trying to make a life in the circus."

In the afternoon, we try out the German wheel—two interconnected metal wheels that are bigger than any of us. Usually, I'd be excited. Today, I'm...well, a little afraid. If those wheels fell on one of us...I stop myself. I'm beginning to think like my dad.

"I get dizzy just looking at that contraption," Guillaume says.

"Put one finger on the tip of your nose, like this"—I demonstrate for Guillaume—"and stare at a fixed point."

Hana is still carting around that library book about circus history. She flips to the page about the German wheel and reads from it, slowly, enunciating every word. "*The German wheel was invented by Otto Feick, a railroad maker, who was imprisoned in the 1920s in Germany, but many people believe the German wheel originated long before then as an instrument of torture.* Oh my." Hana slams the book shut.

"Torture? Now why doesn't that surprise me?" Leo asks with a laugh.

Everyone laughs except Genevieve and me. I don't think it's only because we're still upset about Louise's death. I think it's also because we both feel Leo was playing with us. Maybe that's what happens when you feel disappointed by someone who is funny—his jokes stop working on you.

The acrobatics coach shows us how to step into the German wheel and how to use the footboards and handgrips. "This is a heavy piece of equipment, and it accelerates quickly," he warns. "So you need to know how to keep it stable. Also, make sure your shoelaces are tightly tied—you don't want them catching on the apparatus."

Catching on the apparatus. Already I'm picturing that happening—the shoelace coming loose, the German wheel falling, the performer trying to pull his leg out of the way but not being able to. Stop it, I tell myself. Concentrate on the lesson.

The coach gestures for us to give him some room, and then, because we ask him to show us something fancy, he demonstrates an advanced move: the spiral. He leans into the wheel until it's hovering over the floor. It's hard to tell where his body ends and the German wheel begins. The two swirl so quickly, it's like watching a dropped coin spin to the ground. When he's done, the coach steps out of the wheel as if he's stepping off the bus. How can he not be dizzy?

Anastasia is the first to try the wheel. The coach wants her to get into something called the stride stand position. "Stand tall," he tells her, though he doesn't have to because Anastasia always stands tall. Standing tall must be a Bershov family trait.

"Straight legs! Toes over the edge of the footboards!" The coach nods at Anastasia, then turns to the rest of us. "See how her body is centered inside the wheel."

We won't be doing any spirals today—the first lesson is just getting into proper position, then rocking the wheel from side to side. It doesn't take long before the sweat is dripping down Anastasia's cheeks.

Suzanne walks into the gym carrying a folded-up sheet of paper. She and the coach exchange a quick look. Like Terence, Suzanne has also begun to look older to me since we got the news of Louise's death. "Anastasia," Suzanne says, "I need to speak with you, please. Privately."

Anastasia must sense something is wrong. She inhales sharply and follows Suzanne out of the gym.

We all turn to watch, even though we know it would be more polite to give Anastasia some privacy. Suzanne closes the gym doors behind her. She doesn't want us to hear whatever it is she's come to talk to Anastasia about.

Only seconds later, Anastasia cries out—just once, but loudly.

Oh no, I think. More bad news.

Genevieve, Hana and I are up on our feet. The acrobatics coach extends his arm like a traffic cop. I can see from his face that he's trying to decide whether to let us go to Anastasia.

But we're already going. We don't have to ask Anastasia what has happened because as soon as she sees us, her face crumples and she whispers, "My father had a heart attack. I'm going home."

Anastasia goes upstairs to pack. She is leaving for Moscow tonight.

"But she won't be here for the end-of-camp show," Genevieve says.

"For a girl," Hana tells Genevieve, "her father is the most important man."

* * *

Later, after Anastasia has said a tearful goodbye to all of us, my cell phone rings. "Hi, Mom," I say. "What's up?"

But it isn't my mom. It's my dad. "Dad, why are you call—" I stop myself when I realize how that must sound. "Hey, Dad, how're things in Vancouver?"

"Mandy."

I know from the way he says my name that he's heard about the aerialist who died. He's probably going to tell me to take the next plane home.

"I just read on the Internet about the young woman with Cirque Viva who fell to her death," Dad says.

"I'm not coming home." Even though there are thirty-one hundred miles between us, I can feel my body bracing for a fight. Probably because I'm so used to fighting with my dad. "They think a carabiner broke. It was a freak accident."

"That isn't why I'm calling."

It takes me a moment to register what my dad just said. "It isn't?"

"No, it isn't. Your mom is out at Pilates and, well...I just wanted to know how you were doing. How you were taking the news of...what happened." I know Dad is trying to avoid saying the words *fell* and *death* again.

I feel my shoulders relax. "I'm okay, I guess. A lot of people here knew the woman who died. Louise. She went to MCC. My climbing coach, Terence—he trained with her. They're flying the flag across the street at half-mast." I'm babbling.

And I haven't answered my dad's question. "I guess the news hasn't really sunk in yet."

"Just promise me you'll be careful," Dad says.

"I'm always careful." I don't mean for the words to come out sounding sharp, but they do.

I could apologize for my tone, but changing the subject is easier. "This other girl at camp, Anastasia, she's flying home to Moscow tonight. Her father had a heart attack."

"I'm sorry to hear it. Is he going to be all right?"

"They don't know yet."

I nearly tell him Anastasia is from a famous Russian circus family, but I stop myself. Dad won't think it's cool the way I do.

I can hear the TV in the background. "You watching baseball?"

"Uh-huh."

"I should probably get off the phone." This may be the longest conversation I've had with my dad all year.

"Mandy." The way he says my name sounds different than it did before. "The aerialist's death... it's bringing up a lot of stuff for me. Memories of your grandfather's death. I think that's why I needed to know how you were doing—how you were handling the news."

"Like I said, it hasn't really sunk in. Was it like that for you too?" It's the first time I've ever pictured my dad as a teenager.

Instead of answering my question, Dad does something that takes me by surprise. He tells me a part of the story I've never heard before. "Your grandmother was too upset to go to the morgue to identify the body. So I had to go instead."

There's a lump forming in my throat. "Oh, Dad," I say. "That's so sad. And you were just a kid, right?"

I know my dad must be remembering—picturing the scene at the morgue. "I was fifteen," he says. "The same age as you are now. Just tell me you'll be careful."

"We already had this conversation."

When I hang up, I feel relieved the call is over—and irritated with my dad. Why does he have to keep dumping all his worry on me?

It isn't until later that I wish I hadn't snapped at him.

Fourteen

Terence isn't in la palestre when we show up for aerial class on Tuesday morning. While we wait, Genevieve hoists her feet up against the wall and starts doing these killer push-ups. I could do them too, but I don't want to look like I'm copying her. Besides, I don't think I could handle more than six of those things.

Genevieve does three sets of twelve before she collapses spread-eagle on the mats. "I had a nightmare last night," she says without looking up at me. "About the aerialist who died. You having nightmares too?"

"Not so far," I tell her. "But I keep picturing it...the carabiner breaking, the rope slipping loose..."

Genevieve sits up and looks right at me. "There must've been something wrong with the carabiner," she says.

Terence is ten minutes late. "Sorry, ladies," he calls from the doorway. I've never seen him in a suit and tie before. He looks more like a bank manager than an aerial instructor.

"How come you're all dressed up?" Genevieve asks.

I nudge her. She may be better than I am at doing push-ups, but she's not so good at figuring stuff out. I look at her and mouth the word *funeral*.

"Oh my god," Genevieve blurts out, "you were at the funeral! How was it?"

"Awful." I can tell it's hard for Terence to look at us. "Louise has a two-year-old daughter. *Had*," he corrects himself.

He goes to his office to change into his tracksuit. "Look," he says when he comes out, "I'd rather not talk about the funeral. But I need to talk to you two about the accident."

"There was something wrong with the carabiner, wasn't there?" Genevieve says.

Terence nods. "That's what it looks like."

Genevieve turns to me. "I told you so."

Why does being right matter so much to her?

"There's going to be an investigation," Terence tells us. "But yes, at this point it looks like the carabiner was defective. The carabiner holding Louise's rope was made of aluminum. If someone drops an aluminum carabiner, it can develop micro fissures. The carabiners here are made of steel." Terence looks up at the ceiling of la palestre, where the carabiners are attached to straps hooked around giant beams. "They're 100 percent unbreakable. So you never have to worry about something like that happening here." He sighs. "Are you two ready to get back to work—or do you want to talk about this some more?"

"We're ready," Genevieve answers for both of us.

Some hair has come loose from Terence's ponytail, and he tucks it back behind his ear. "I was thinking," he says, and I get the feeling he's glad not to have to talk anymore about what happened to his friend Louise, "we only have five classes together before Friday's final performance. Our focus needs to shift from reviewing basics to creating acts that will dazzle an audience."

Genevieve and I will be training side by side, Genevieve on tissu, me on the rope.

Terence wants Genevieve to work on her splits. I've seen her do them before. With her heels triple wrapped, each in a separate tissu, arms bent at the elbows, holding on to the two pieces of fabric, Genevieve extends her arms and opens into the splits. But Terence means what he said about creating acts that will dazzle an audience. "Today," he tells Genevieve, "you're only going to hold on to one piece of the tissu—with both hands, of course. I want to see a nice arch in your back. We're stepping up the technical difficulty and working on your balance."

Genevieve is already climbing up the tissu, eager to try the new move.

Terence makes her come back down to the mats. "Hey, hey," he says, "not so fast. I appreciate your enthusiasm, but I need to be able to watch both of you at the same time." Then he turns to me. "Mandy, I think you're ready to try the starfish."

"Okay." I look away for a second because I don't want Terence or Genevieve to know I'm a little nervous. Usually I can't wait to try out a new move. But not today. Maybe Louise's death has spooked me.

"Mandy?" Terence says. "You with me?"

He must have noticed my hesitation. "I'm with you," I tell him.

The starfish is sometimes called the catcher's baby drop. If you ask me, it looks even more dramatic than Genevieve's splits.

Terence reviews the move with me step by step. The starfish starts with an inverted lock, which will keep me hanging securely upside down. "As soon as you put your leg on the rope," Terence says, "you'll need to lift your hips up over your hands. Then you reach overhead to find the tail of the rope, wrap the rope around the inside of your leg, release your hand in the groin and let your body hang straight down. After that, you pass the rope around your waist. That will be your inverted lock. Then you extend your arms and legs and you've got your starfish."

I close my eyes and try picturing the move in my head. But then I see the carabiner—the shards of aluminum exploding in the air.

Terence is still explaining. "It's important to maintain body tension," he says, "if you want to get the star shape right."

"Body tension is the one thing you don't have to teach Mandy," Genevieve says. "That girl is tense all the time." Then she catches my eye and adds, "Just kidding!"

I try to think of a quick comeback, but Terence beats me to it. "You know something, Genevieve? A little tension isn't always a bad thing in a circus performer. Sometimes it's the ones who are too cocky and too confident who get into trouble. And the ones who are a little tense and a little less confident end up working harder and sometimes become the real stars of circus."

Genevieve shrugs. "Can we start climbing now?"

She is at the top of the tissu before I am halfway up my rope. I keep my eyes on the rope and on my hands. At least I'm not still imagining the broken carabiner.

"What do you think? Am I going to wow the audience?" Genevieve calls down to Terence.

I know a little competition can be a good thing, that it pushes us to work harder, but Genevieve takes competition to a whole other level.

"Good foot lock," Terence calls back to her.

At this rate, Genevieve will have done her advanced splits before I'm even at the top of the rope. I try to resist the urge to watch what she is doing. I don't want to lose time. I also don't want to give Genevieve the satisfaction. But when Terence calls out, "Very nice!" I go into a resting position, locking the rope around my hips and releasing my arms. I look up and there is Genevieve—doing perfect splits, arching her back and holding on to just one piece of the tissu. How did she manage to get the move right on her first try?

When she sees me watching her, she lifts one hand off the tissu and waves.

Terence isn't chuckling anymore. "Concentrate, Genevieve!" he shouts. "Both hands on the tissu! Now!"

I'm high enough up by this time to try the starfish. I don't know why my heart is thumping in my chest. Calm down, I tell myself. Concentrate...

Louise. It's the aerialist's name that comes to me now, not the picture of the shattered carabiner.

"Show me that starfish!" Terence calls.

I've done the inverted lock before, but today I struggle with it. Instead of reaching overhead to find the tail of the rope, I reach behind my back.

When I try to correct myself, I slip a little on the rope. Even the powdery rosin I've put on my hands doesn't catch all my sweat.

With my head inverted, I can look right down at Terence. Our eyes meet, and he nods. "Good correction!" he says.

I can feel Terence watching, concentrating, as I bring the rope in front of my body. I'm ready now to move into the starfish. The rope feels secure around my waist and thigh. I breathe deeply as I extend my arms. There, I think, I've done it.

But I haven't. This time, Genevieve, who is resting on her tissu, is the one who corrects me. "You've still got one knee bent over the rope, silly!" she calls.

I unbend my knee and extend the leg. My hands and feet are pointed, and I'm maintaining body tension the way Terence told me to. For a few moments, I am not Mandy. I am a starfish. A starfish who isn't afraid of anything.

Genevieve goes a little deeper into the splits.

As for me, I review all the steps involved in the starfish in my head. In my imagination, I get all of them right. But in real life, I keep making new mistakes. I unhook my knee from the rope, but I don't bring the rope right to the front of my body. Or I forget to wrap my thigh with the rope before wrapping my waist.

On the ground, Terence is making a T with his arms, signaling that he wants me to take a time-out. "Look at your wrap," he calls up to me, "and see what you're doing wrong." Which is when I realize I've let my knee come off the rope.

"It's only Tuesday," Terence says once I've made the correction. "Your body needs time to integrate what you're learning."

Is it my imagination, or does Terence look at me funny when he says that? Does he know it isn't only my body that needs time to integrate, but my mind too?

And how come Genevieve's body integrates what we're learning more quickly than mine does?

Terence tilts his head and looks at both of us. "All right, girls, back to the mats. A few minutes of cool-down exercises and we'll be done for today."

I concentrate on my technique as I slide down the rope. I know Terence is still watching us. When I extend my shoulders, I can feel my deltoids getting a good stretch. All this is part of the performance too.

I hear someone say "Oh!" Genevieve was swinging on the tissu and has caught her ankle on the fabric. I watch as she tries to kick it loose. Even without looking at Terence, I know he is moving in closer to her, in case she needs his help.

But Genevieve's ankle is still caught.

"Wait! I'm coming!" Terence tells her.

But Genevieve won't wait. I can feel her frustration as she kicks at the tissu, harder each time. And then, only seconds later, Genevieve slips, and I hear a *thud* as part of her lands on the mats. And part of her doesn't.

Oh my god. Is she all right?

I'm down on the mats now too. My heart feels like it's beating in my throat. "Genevieve!"

Genevieve yelps in pain when she tries to get up. She drops back on the mats, clutching her ankle. Tears are streaming down her cheeks, and I've never seen her look so pale or so frightened.

Terence crouches on the floor next to Genevieve. "Get Suzanne! Now! Tell her we need an ambulance!" he barks.

The hallway is a blur.

I can hardly breathe when I get to Suzanne's desk. She must know something is wrong. "What is it?" she asks.

My tongue feels frozen, but I manage to get the words out. "We need an ambulance. Genevieve fell."

Suzanne's eyes are on me as she dials 9-1-1. "Is she conscious?" she asks.

"Yes."

Suzanne sighs. "Thank God."

I hear the whine of the ambulance before I am back in la palestre. Genevieve's eyes are closed, and she's still clutching her ankle. "I won't be able to finish circus ca—" she starts to say when she sees me. But she must be in too much pain to finish her sentence. She whimpers when two paramedics rush into la palestre. They examine her, then load her onto a stretcher.

"It looks like a broken ankle," I hear one of the paramedics tell Terence and Suzanne. "They'll want to do an x-ray."

Terence and I watch from the window as the paramedics hoist the stretcher into the back of the ambulance. Suzanne gets into the ambulance too.

Terence shakes his head. "Let's hope it's just her ankle," he says. Then he turns to me. "Anastasia is gone, and now Genevieve too. That means we're down to one aerialist for Friday's show. And we only have three more days to perfect your routine."

Fifteen

On Wednesday morning in la palestre, it's just Terence, me and the rope.

I'm practicing the starfish on the mats, and he's pointing out everything that needs fixing. "Spread out your fingers—that'll add to the effect" and "I want you to feel the tension, even in your knees." La palestre seems eerily quiet without Genevieve. I look over at the tissu hanging limply from the ceiling, and for a moment I lose track of what Terence is telling me. I didn't realize how much I'd miss Genevieve and her wisecracks.

I'm doing my best, but I can't help thinking that if Genevieve were up on the tissu, I'd be working even harder. From the time we met—

it's hard to believe it was only a little over a week ago—almost everything Genevieve has said or done has annoyed me, but now I see that her influence has not been all bad. Training next to someone as good as Genevieve has motivated me to try and push past my own limits.

"What if she'd hit her head?" I say to Terence when he gives me a short break.

Terence bites his lip. "I've been thinking that too. Things could have been a lot worse. But even if it's just her ankle, it'll be months before she can do tissu again."

Which means Genevieve may not be able to apply to MCC next spring. Which, of course, seriously improves my chances of being accepted. I should be happy, only I'm not. I feel empty, as if a part of me is missing.

"Is Genevieve going home to Seattle?" I ask Terence.

"I would think so. Suzanne went back to the hospital first thing this morning. Last I heard, the swelling is down, so Genevieve will probably get her cast today. Once that's done, she should be comfortable enough to fly."

"But then we won't be able to say goodbye to her."

"I'm afraid not." Terence gives me a puzzled look. "I didn't realize you two were so close."

"We aren't. I mean, we weren't..." I picture Genevieve on the tissu, smirking down at me. "Being around someone so talented pushed me to work even harder." It's the closest I can get to explaining to Terence why it feels wrong not to be able to say goodbye to Genevieve.

"I know what you mean," Terence says. "It's how I felt about Louise."

"I'm really sorry about what happened to her." I don't know why I didn't think of saying this before. Maybe I've been too caught up in my own feelings.

"Thanks," Terence says. "I appreciate it."

I hear clattering noises outside la palestre. Terence and I both turn to look toward the sound.

The door swings open and there, leaning on a metal crutch, her right foot in a cast, is Genevieve. She is using the other crutch to hold the door open.

I jog over to meet her. "Genevieve! How's your ankle?"

Genevieve lifts her ankle to show me her cast. "It's broken in two places. I have to stay off it for at least a month. Can you imagine anything more boring? But the good news is the doctors don't think I'll need surgery." Her eyes are less bright than usual. She probably didn't get much sleep at the hospital, or maybe she's on painkillers.

"I can't believe you're here. Terence was just saying he thought you'd be flying home today."

"Flying back to Seattle today? No way!" Genevieve rolls her eyes. "It would cost my parents a bundle if they had to change my ticket. So you're stuck with me till the end of circus camp." Her voice turns serious. "Besides, there's no way I'm missing the final performance on Friday."

"I'm glad," I tell her. "I'd have felt bad if we didn't get a chance to say goodbye."

"Those aren't the only reasons I came back," Genevieve says.

Terence has brought over a chair for Genevieve. He helps her to sit down and props her crutches up next to her. "What's the other reason?" he asks.

"Well, I was thinking...now that I can't train, I came up with another plan to keep me busy." Genevieve looks from me to Terence, then back to me. "I figured I could help coach you, Mandy. That is"—she turns to Terence again—"if you're okay with that."

It's the first time I've seen Terence smile since we heard about Louise's death. "Of course I'm okay with it," he says. "I think it's very generous of you. And keeping busy like that will be good for you, Genevieve. If you really think you're up for it."

"I'm up for it."

I haven't said a word. That's because I don't know what to say. If the situation were reversed, I'd never, ever offer to help train Genevieve.

"So, what do you say, Mandy?" she asks.

I should probably say thank you, but I don't. "Why would you do that for me?"

Genevieve doesn't answer. Instead, she has another question. "Wouldn't you do it for me?"

More clattering outside la palestre saves me from having to tell a lie. It's Leo and Guillaume. Where did they find skateboards?

"Hey, hey, boys! Be careful of the floors in here!" Terence tries to block them from entering la palestre, but they skate right around him and over to Genevieve.

Leo is holding a bouquet of flowers in one hand. The flowers aren't wrapped in plastic the way they would be if they were from a flower shop or the supermarket, and the assortment—pink and red petunias, yellow marigolds—pretty much confirms he picked them from a flower box on the terrace.

"Genevieve," Leo says, stepping off his skateboard to present her with the bouquet, "these flowers are for you...for your convalescence."

Genevieve takes the flowers and presses them to her nose.

Leo and Guillaume get back on their skateboards. They wiggle their butts and wave their hands in the air. This time, even Terence chuckles.

Sixteen

G*rrr!* I'll never get the hang of juggling! After practicing for more than a week, I still can't keep two balls in the air.

Hana can juggle three balls. In fact, I think she's getting obsessed. Yesterday she asked permission to borrow three squishy balls so she could practice in the dorm. When I got up to pee last night, she was juggling on her bed. Who knew juggling could be an antidote for homesickness?

Now Hana is juggling those balls so quickly, I can't keep track of which is which.

"You're getting really good," I tell her.

Hana is better at juggling than at accepting compliments. "I think it's because I have aptitude for mathematics."

"I don't know what math has to do with it."

Genevieve, who is sitting on another folding chair, insists on juggling too. Suzanne is not so sure that is a good idea, but as we all know by now, Genevieve can be very stubborn. "Besides," she tells Suzanne, "no one said I had to rest my *upper* body."

Suzanne gives in, maybe because she is worn out from having gone back and forth to the hospital and having attended Louise's funeral.

When Genevieve drops one of her squishy balls and it rolls along the floor, I take off after it. It's only when Genevieve misses four or five catches in a row that I realize she's doing it on purpose. She bursts into laughter when I toss the squishy ball in her face. "I wondered how long it would take you to figure that out," she says.

I'm back on the floor, throwing my two balls up into the air, still trying to get the timing right, when I feel Suzanne standing next to me. She doesn't say anything, just watches as I struggle to keep the balls moving. "You need to concentrate—and relax," she says.

"I am concentrating!" I manage to say it without taking my eyes off the ball.

"But you're not relaxed, are you?"

Suzanne walks off before I can answer. I miss my catch, and the ball brushes against the side of my face before landing on the mat. *Grrr!*

I know Suzanne is right. But concentrating and being relaxed at the same time is harder than it sounds.

A few minutes later, I get up to use the water fountain—not only because I'm thirsty, but also because I need a break from my own bad juggling. Suzanne is getting water too. "I was just wondering," I say to her. "Isn't concentrating the opposite of being relaxed?"

Suzanne pats my shoulder. "Not in circus it isn't."

It doesn't help my juggling to think how learning to juggle even three balls would help my chances of being accepted into MCC. Versatility is one of the qualities the selection committee looks for in performers. When I start thinking about that, I mess up even worse. So much for feeling relaxed.

For the next couple of minutes, I just lie on my mat and breathe deeply—in and out, in and out, over and over again. I relax my shoulders and arms, which are tense from juggling—or in my case, trying to juggle. With eyes closed, I reach for my two squishy balls. Then I open my eyes and toss one ball up into the air. I'm relaxed and concentrating, really I am.

When the ball is just starting to arc, I toss up the second ball. And then something miraculous and magical happens: I'm juggling. I'm so excited I nearly shout out loud that I've done it, that I'm doing it, but I don't because I'm afraid to break the spell.

* * *

Mom calls that evening. "You sound good," she says. I don't know how Mom can read my moods even over the phone.

"I'm learning to juggle. I've been trying to do it for over a week, but today I finally started to get the hang of it."

Mom laughs. "That's wonderful! I can't wait to see you, Mandy."

The plan is for her to fly to Montreal on Friday in time to catch our final performance. My dad isn't coming.

"Dad told me about the morgue," I say.

Mom knows right away what I mean. "I was a little surprised he did that. In all the years we've been married, he's hardly ever mentioned his father and what happened."

I'm thinking about Grandpa. Would my life have been different if I'd known him? It's hard for me to imagine that my serious, conservative engineer father could be the son of a stuntman. "Why do you think he doesn't talk about his dad?"

I can almost hear Mom thinking on the other end of the phone. "I think it's partly because he was so traumatized by his death."

"I know he was pretty shook up about the news of that aerialist's death. He told me it brought back a lot of memories. I guess he's afraid I'll get hurt—or die—in some accident too." I was going to tell Mom about Genevieve's broken ankle, but I decide this isn't a good time.

"You're right that he worries about you getting hurt, Mandy. But there's more to it. I think he hasn't wanted to burden you."

"Burden me?" Now I'm confused. "Why would it burden me? I wasn't even born when it happened."

"You know, Mandy, when you were little, you were like a little monkey." Mom's voice softens, and I know it's because she's remembering. Sometimes I think she misses having a little girl around.

"I don't think you were ever so happy as when you were climbing a tree. Your father worried, I know he did, but at the same time, he didn't want to take that joy away from you. Looking back now, I see it was very generous of him."

There's that word again. *Generous.* First Genevieve, and now my father. What I can't figure out is why the two people who've been most generous with me lately are the last two people I ever expected it from.

Seventeen

On Thursday morning, I happen to pass the ground-floor studios. In one, students are working on contortion exercises. They're doing the pretzel, their backs arched, their palms pressing down on the floor behind them. One boy's body shakes from the strain. I hope that won't happen to him during our performance tomorrow.

I pause in front of the next studio. Hugo Lebrun is hunched forward on a stool, his chin resting on his hand like the guy in that famous sculpture by Rodin. He is watching Leo and Guillaume rehearse the routine they'll be doing for the final performance.

Both boys are wearing plaid pajamas—Leo's are red; Guillaume's are blue. They're not wearing clown noses, but they have huge gray felt slippers that make walking difficult.

Guillaume nearly trips over his slippers, but Leo catches him just in time, only to fall over backward. Then Guillaume trips over Leo and falls to a heap on the floor. The two boys raise their legs in the air, waving their slippers in Hugo's direction. It's a silly gag, but I still laugh, because it's *so* silly.

They're working with props today. There's a narrow metal cot with a mattress on it, a huge washing machine and dryer, both made out of cardboard spray-painted a glossy white, and a pink wicker laundry basket.

Leo drags Guillaume up from the floor and marches him over to the cardboard dryer. He points at it, gesturing that he wants Guillaume to unload what's inside, then taps his wrist where a watch would be.

Guillaume nods obediently. He's leaning down to reach into the dryer when Leo pulls open the dryer door, smacking him in the forehead. Guillaume falls over backward, taking the opportunity to do a somersault.

Leo lifts him up from the floor and dusts him off as if he's a piece of furniture. Then he points back at the dryer.

This time Guillaume reaches in and begins pulling out a white bedsheet...and pulling...and pulling. The sheet has to be at least ten bedsheets sewn together. Leo is pointing at the bed now and looking again at his wrist. He wants Guillaume to make the bed. Now!

Of course, when Guillaume finally gets the sheet out, it is way too big for one bed. He and Leo get tangled up inside it. Gray slippers emerge from under the giant sheet.

Leo hands Guillaume the laundry basket. Guillaume pulls out several men's dress shirts. Then he pulls out a lacy pink nightgown, waving it in front of Leo.

Leo bonks the side of Guillaume's head. The nightgown drops out of Guillaume's hands, landing back in the laundry basket.

Leo points at the cardboard washing machine and checks the time again.

Guillaume trips over the basket. He stumbles to his feet, stuffs the shirts into the washing machine, then pulls them out and stuffs them into the dryer.

Leo points at his red-plaid pajama top. He needs a clean shirt! Guillaume dabs his forehead with the back of his hand. When he reaches into the dryer and sees what is inside, he stops, then turns to look back at the audience—Hugo, and me too, though Guillaume doesn't seem to notice I am standing at the window. Just his expression—his eyebrows shoot up in a combination of surprise and horror—cracks me up.

Guillaume reaches again into the dryer and pulls out six tiny white shirts and a tiny lacy pink nightgown, all too small even for a doll.

Leo's eyes widen. Then he starts chasing Guillaume around the studio. They go in circles, banging into each other and tripping over the bed, the laundry basket and their oversized slippers. They collapse on the floor, then get up and start all over again.

Leo finally catches Guillaume and stuffs him inside the dryer. Leo is turning the pretend dial on the dryer when Guillaume pops his head out of the dryer door.

The two boys are having so much fun, they both start laughing. Leo laughs so hard he has to hold on to his side.

Hugo gets up from his stool. He wags his finger at the boys, and though I can't hear what he is saying, I know he is telling Leo and Guillaume they must stay in character until the very end of their performance.

I watch as Leo and Guillaume nod solemnly. Hugo knows that they are talented, but he's pushing them to become even better and more professional—the way that Terence has been pushing Genevieve and me.

I think back to what Anastasia said—how the most important part of being a circus performer is connecting with your audience. That's what Leo and Guillaume are so good at. It's something I have to keep working on in my own way. That's because connecting with the audience is a skill no circus instructor, even one as famous as Hugo Lebrun, can teach.

Eighteen

Having Genevieve as my assistant coach is almost as bad as having her as my rival.

She's bossy and stubborn—and she doesn't listen.

"It's not enough for Mandy to do cool moves on the rope," she tells Terence. Genevieve has two chairs now: one for sitting, the other for resting her foot. "She needs a story, a narrative, a choreography. I was thinking Tarzana. A female Tarzan. Strong, yet feminine."

"Hey, you looking to take over my job here?" Terence asks.

Genevieve misses Terence's joke. She is still babbling about the Tarzana choreography. "We'd have to give it a jungle feel," she says. "I was thinking Mandy could wear a leopard-print leotard..."

It bothers me that she's talking about me as if I'm not there. "I don't think so," I say, but neither Genevieve nor Terence seems to notice that I've said something.

I clear my throat. "I don't think so." This time I raise my voice, and the two of them look at me.

Genevieve looks like she's surprised to see me in la palestre. "What don't you think?"

"Genevieve is right," Terence says. "I was planning to talk to you about choreography ideas this morning, Mandy. The Tarzana theme isn't a bad—"

"Tarzana, the jungle, the leopard-print leotard...none of it is me," I tell them. "Besides, I have my own idea."

"What?" Genevieve and Terence ask at the same time.

"I was thinking spider. I could use the rope for my web."

Genevieve does not give up easily. "I planned out your whole Tarzana routine. You could start by swinging on the rope, the way Tarzan—"

Luckily, Terence cuts her off. "I'm liking the spider," he says. "I'm liking it a lot."

There is only one day before the final performance. Genevieve thinks the background music should be dark and haunting. But I want something lighter, more fun. "I've got it—'Itsy Bitsy Spider,'" I tell Genevieve and Terence.

Genevieve rolls her eyes. "Let me get this straight. You're fifteen years old and you want to perform your number to a nursery rhyme?"

"Yup. Ever heard of Carly Simon? She does a great version. My parents had the CD. 'Itsy Bitsy Spider' is still one of my all-time favorite songs."

Terence closes his eyes, then opens them again. "I think you're on to something, Mandy." He hands Genevieve a pen and notepad. "Why don't you take notes while we brainstorm? So we don't forget anything important."

I think it's Terence's way to keep Genevieve busy—and quiet. Temporarily anyway.

We discuss my routine and how we can tie it into the "Itsy Bitsy Spider" song. Terence gets his laptop from his office, and we listen to Carly Simon's version.

"Why are you smiling like that?" Genevieve asks.

I didn't realize I was smiling. "I was just remembering how my dad used to tickle my arm when the spider went up the water spout. Then he'd wave when the sun came out."

We decide that I'll do my basic climb matching my pace to Carly Simon's rhythm. Then I'll straddle the rope, do splits and go into the starfish when the sun comes out in the song.

Genevieve looks up from her notepad. "I just thought of something! What about flowerpots and a garden hose on the ground, to tie into the garden theme? We could get the maintenance crew to bring in some of the flowerpots from the terrace. I saw a hose out there too."

Terence and I like those ideas. Terence tells us that his girlfriend is a set designer and that he'll ask for her input too.

I agree with Terence that the performance shouldn't end with me doing the starfish. "At the end of the song, the spider goes up the rope again. Maybe I should end with my toes spread in a toe climb, or one knee bent sideways for the knee hook climb."

Terence's cell phone rings. It must be his girlfriend, because he asks her opinion about the stage setup for my performance. "Girls," he tells us, "I need a few minutes." He walks to his office, holding his cell phone to his ear.

"I was thinking..." Genevieve says when Terence is out of earshot.

"What were you thinking?"

"That if you really want your performance to pop...if you really want it to be the part of the show the audience never forgets, you should end your act with—" Genevieve stops, as if she's decided it isn't a good idea to say whatever she was about to say.

"With what?"

"Nah, nothing."

"Come on, Genevieve! Tell me!"

"Nah, forget it."

"Genevieve!"

"I was going to say you should end your act with a triple star roll."

"A triple star roll? The move where you spiral down the rope three times? I don't think I could do that."

Genevieve smiles. It's a small, knowing smile. "You're probably right," she says. "You couldn't do it."

The smug way Genevieve says it makes me decide something right then and there. Not only do I want to learn the triple star roll, but I want to use it for the finale of my performance tomorrow.

Nineteen

There's a mattress coming at me. And another one behind it.

I know from the sneakers sticking out from underneath that it's Leo and Guillaume pushing the mattresses down the corridor.

The corridor is wide, but the mattresses are wider. The boys have to angle them sideways, which is why they don't see me.

"Hey, hey, watch out," I say. "We're already down two performers for Friday. What are you doing with those things anyhow?"

Guillaume peeks out from behind his mattress. "Haven't you heard? Tonight is the Perseid meteor shower. It's going to be a hundred times better than fireworks. We're bringing our mattresses out so we can watch from the terrace. We're coming to the girls' dormitory afterward and getting your mattresses too."

Hana has walked up behind me. "Boys are not allowed in the girls' dormitory," she says.

Now it's Leo's turn to peek out from behind the mattress he is carrying. "Well then, we'll stand outside and you can pass us your mattresses. This is one show you don't want to miss."

"I think we're going to need popcorn," I tell the boys.

"Do you think you can get the cheese-flavored kind?" Guillaume asks.

Since cheese-flavored popcorn falls into the junk-food category, there isn't any in the cafeteria. So Hana comes with me to the dépanneur on Jarry Street to buy three bags. When we get back to the girls' dorm, Leo and Guillaume are inside, taking the mattresses off the bunk beds.

Because it's Leo and Guillaume, they turn it into a performance. Guillaume climbs up to Genevieve's bunk and throws down the mattress. Leo bounces on the mattress, then does a double somersault.

Guillaume crosses his hands over his chest when he sees Hana. "Look out! The Korean police are here!"

Genevieve must have gone to the bathroom, but now she is hobbling back into the room. "Put my mattress back this instant," she says.

"Don't you want to see the meteor shower with the rest of us?" Guillaume asks.

"What meteor shower?"

Leo bends down on one knee in front of Genevieve. "It's going to be the best stargazing night of the whole summer! Come on—it'll be fun! Suzanne gave us permission."

"Fine!" Genevieve says. "I'll watch the meteor shower. Just don't put my mattress next to yours." She looks up at Leo and then at Guillaume. "Or his!"

* * *

At a quarter to eleven, we are all lying on our mattresses on the terrace. Leo and Guillaume have pushed them together to make one giant mattress. We've each brought a pillow and, because the night air has a slight chill to it, our blankets too.

In the distance, we can hear the *whoosh* of cars and trucks on the Metropolitan Highway. But the crickets are even louder, chirping to each other in the grassy field next to the MCC.

I yawn, which sets off a chain reaction of yawning.

The door that leads from the school to the terrace swings open. Suzanne shines her flashlight on the middle of the terrace. "With all the yawning going on," she says, "I don't know if you guys will be awake to see any shooting stars." Then Suzanne yawns too, and we all laugh at her.

"I know one person who definitely won't be awake," Leo calls out.

Even Suzanne laughs. "All right then, all of you. Enjoy the show—and when it's over, get those mattresses back inside. You've got another early morning tomorrow."

"Can't we sleep out here under the stars? Just this once?" Guillaume asks.

Suzanne looks up at the sky. "I wish I could say yes," she says. "But regulations are regulations."

As if on cue, at exactly midnight the Perseid meteor shower begins. It starts with streaks of silvery light. One fades and then, not long afterward, another appears. Soon there are more of them, and they come more frequently. "Wow!" Hana says.

Even Genevieve is enjoying herself. "It really is like fireworks!" she says.

Guillaume is the only who has dozed off, his head slumped on Leo's shoulder.

Leo tries to shake him loose. "Wake up! You're missing the show!"

Guillaume groans but doesn't wake up.

"You know what would be really cool?" Leo says to the rest of us. "Watching the showers from up there." He lifts his eyes to the maple tree behind the terrace.

He's right—the view from the top of that tree would be amazing.

Leo turns to me. "I bet you could climb up there."

"I bet I could." The maple tree is about the same height as the tree behind our house in North Vancouver. It's got a tall trunk with plenty of thick branches. It wouldn't be hard to climb.

Leo slides his arm out from behind Guillaume's shoulder. Then he stands up and offers me his hand. "You coming?"

Genevieve bangs her cast on the edge of her mattress. "I miss climbing," she mutters. "I'd do it if I could."

Hana puts her hand on my forearm. "You should not do it," she says. "It's against the rules to practice without supervision. Suzanne told us so. If someone gets hurt, the camp will be sued."

Guillaume is awake now. "What's going on?" he asks sleepily.

"Leo and Mandy are about to do a tree-climbing performance for us." Genevieve claps her hands.

Leo is tugging on my arm. "Let's go."

"That isn't cool," Guillaume tells him.

"It's very cool," Leo says.

"If Suzanne finds out, you might get kicked out of circus camp. Then what happens to me?" Guillaume says.

"Suzanne isn't going to find out. You saw her yawning before. I'll bet you anything she's fast asleep, dreaming about rules and regulations," Leo says. He drops my hand. "I see a perfect perch up there for the two of us."

It's hard for me to resist getting caught up in Leo's excitement.

"If it weren't for this cast, I'd climb that tree," Genevieve says.

"What if you get hurt?" Guillaume asks Leo. "Then what?"

When Guillaume says that, I see the shattered carabiner again. Guillaume's right. It's too risky. It's a big jump from the railing to the tree. If one of us falls, there won't be a mat underneath to land on.

"Don't do it," I tell Leo, but he's already gone.

He jumps up onto the railing, takes a deep breath and leaps for the tree. Then he wraps his arms and legs around the maple's trunk and begins hoisting himself up. I can tell right away that he's a good climber.

"Look at him go!" Genevieve exclaims.

Part of me wants to be a kid again and climb that tree with Leo, and show all my friends what a good climber I am. Another part of me knows it's a bad idea.

"Suzanne!" Genevieve calls out.

Leo was wrong about Suzanne being fast asleep. She's come back out to the terrace to check on us again.

"Did you change your mind about seeing the meteor shower?" Genevieve asks.

Guillaume sits up on his mattress and stretches his arms. He's trying to block Genevieve's view of the tree.

"What's going on out here?" Suzanne asks.

Hana's eyes look even bigger than usual. Suzanne must notice that too, because she adds, "Hana, is something wrong?"

If Hana turns Leo in, he'll probably get kicked out of circus camp. And then, of course, his chances—and Guillaume's, too, since they work as a pair—of being accepted into MCC will be affected.

But Hana just shakes her head. "Nothing."

And Suzanne doesn't seem to have noticed that Leo isn't sitting on his mattress anymore.

If it weren't for the shooting star, Leo might have gotten away with it. A silver streak flies by and Suzanne looks up, past Guillaume, to the maple tree next to the terrace. There is Leo, rocking gently on the perch.

"Leo!" Suzanne's voice is sharper than I've ever heard it. "What in God's name are you doing up there? You get yourself down from that tree this instant—and then you report immediately to my office!"

"Come on, Suzanne," Leo says, flashing her a smile from the tree. "Don't be angry. I'm sorry. Can't you be flexible? Just this once?"

"*Flexible*?" Suzanne sounds like she's about to choke on the word. "*Flexible*? You need to be flexible when you're training or performing. But I certainly don't need to be flexible when it comes to enforcing rules at this camp!"

Then Suzanne gives the rest of us a look that lets us know she's disappointed in us too. "As for the rest of you," she says, "this show is officially over. Take those mattresses and get to your dorms! Now!"

Twenty

The next morning, Leo is not having breakfast in the cafeteria.

Guillaume picks at his granola with his spoon. All he will say about Leo is that he's in the boys' dorm. Packing.

The door to Suzanne's office is closed. Genevieve says she spotted Hugo Lebrun going inside earlier. "I'll bet you anything he's trying to talk Suzanne into giving Leo a second chance," she says.

Ten minutes later, Hugo Lebrun struts into the cafeteria and pours himself a coffee, then walks out without even looking at us—and we know Suzanne has not changed her mind.

Hana is sitting across from Guillaume. "How can you do your performance without a partner?" she asks him.

"I've got no friggin' idea." Guillaume spits out the words.

"Friggin'?" Hana wrinkles her forehead. "I never heard that word before. What is its meaning, please?"

Terence doesn't mention Leo, but Genevieve and I know he knows. One sign is that Terence doesn't make any small talk with us. Another is that after I've finished my warm-ups and I put on the "Itsy Bitsy Spider" video, he doesn't hum or tap his fingers the way he did yesterday.

"I've been thinking I'd like to finish my act with a triple star roll," I tell Terence as I'm climbing the rope.

Terence cranes his neck to look at me. "Did I just hear you say *triple star roll*? Because I don't think you're ready for that move, Mandy."

"That's what I told her," Genevieve says.

I hook my elbows around the rope so I can rest for a moment. I look down at Genevieve. "You also told me it would make my performance pop."

Terence shakes his head and looks at Genevieve. "You told her that?"

"Can't I at least try it?" I say.

Terence sighs. "All right then. You can *try* it—but not right away. You're going to have to show me some decent single star rolls first."

The truth is, I haven't had much practice doing single star rolls. The move starts with an inversion. I climb a little higher, then prepare to invert. The rope is hanging at my right side. I lock the rope around my left thigh and then wrap it once around my waist.

"Make sure it's secure!" Terence says.

I tug on the rope. It feels nice and tight around my leg. Soon it's going to be the only thing keeping me up in the air. I take a deep breath.

"Straighten your arms!" Genevieve calls out.

My arms are a little shaky, but I straighten them.

"Begin to straighten your right leg," Terence tells me.

Slowly, carefully, I straighten my leg.

"Your toe!" Terence calls out.

I hook my big toe on the rope.

I take a deep breath and prepare to release. *Thank goodness I'm not thinking about the carabiner.* Only that thought makes me think about it again. *Stop it! Concentrate!*

"Wait!" Terence shouts. "You need to make a bigger straddle! Separate those legs!"

How could I have forgotten that part? I widen my legs.

"That's better! Now take a deep breath—and release your toe!" Terence says.

The second I release my toe, I feel myself beginning to roll down sideways. The sensation is so smooth and floaty, it almost makes me laugh. Down and around I spin until I "land," dangling in the air on my back.

I expect Terence to say I did well, but he doesn't. All he says is "Don't forget to widen your straddle."

He makes me do the move five more times. It isn't easy with Terence barking out instructions. "Rope behind the body, then in front!" "Straight back!" "What did I tell you about your straddle?"

"Extend those arms!" Now it's Genevieve telling me what to do.

"Hey, hey," I hear Terence tell her. "Last time I checked, I was still Mandy's coach. Your job is just to watch."

My leg is getting sore in the spot where I've been cinching the rope. I try not to think about the soreness. Instead, I force myself to concentrate on every step. I know that breaking the move down the way we are doing will help me prepare for the triple star roll. At least, I hope it will.

"All right," Terence finally says, "let's give some double star rolls a try. You're going to follow every one of my instructions. Got that?" Terence has one hand on my shoulder; his eyes are locked on mine.

"Got it!"

I rub my fingers in the bowl of rosin, shake off the residue and start climbing.

"Get ready to invert!" Terence calls when I get near the top of the rope.

My hands tremble a little as I wrap the rope twice around my waist before locking it around my thigh. My hands never used to do that—not even when I was first learning how to do rope. Louise's death has rattled me. Even if I know that a steel carabiner like the one that's keeping my rope attached to the ceiling of la palestre could never shatter the way an aluminum one can. The rattled feeling may not be logical, but I can't shake it. At least, not yet.

I take a deep breath and refocus. I picture myself doing the double star roll, but I know better than to move a muscle. I have to wait for Terence's instructions.

"All right, Mandy, showtime!" he says. "Release that toe!"

The double star roll means I'll be doing a double rotation.

I release my toe.

I've practiced the single star roll so much that the first part of the new move feels almost automatic. The only real difference so far is that the double wrap feels tight around my belly—so tight that I need to arch my back a little. I have to get used to the tightness. I'm looking up at the ceiling, so I can't see Terence or Genevieve, but I know their eyes must be glued to me—and to the rope.

"Don't arch your back!" Terence shouts almost as soon as I begin rolling. "It's poor form. Stay tight! Engage those abs!"

When the second rotation comes to an end and I've dangled from the rope for a bit, I slide down to the mats.

"One more double, and then we'll try the triple star roll," Terence says. "How's your leg? Not too sore?"

"It's fine." I hope Terence can't tell I'm lying.

My second double star roll goes better than my first.

Soon I'm wrapping the rope three times around my waist, then locking it around my thigh for the triple star roll.

I inhale before I straighten my arms and hook my toe on the rope. I think about how circus is a combination of work and play. Right now, though, it feels more like work than play.

This time, the speed at which I spin catches me by surprise. Round and round, then round and round again. Faster. One more time around. Even faster, my speed accumulating with every rotation.

I can hardly believe I'm doing it! The triple star roll!

The feeling of the rope behind me steadies me and keeps me from getting dizzy.

When I finally stop spinning, I'm on my back, grinning so hard at the ceiling that my face hurts. The wrap is still secure around my thigh.

I'm still grinning when I land on the mat. Genevieve reaches over from the chair where she is sitting to clap me on the back. "I knew you could do it!" she says. "No one will ever forget your 'Itsy Bitsy Spider' routine now."

I'm expecting Terence to congratulate me, but he doesn't. Instead, he turns to Genevieve. "You're getting ahead of yourself," he tells her. "And Mandy, you're going to have to practice that move several more times before I consider letting you include it in your act. I'm still seeing too much arch in your back."

"I was just trying to help Mand—"

Terence cuts Genevieve off. "You know something, Genevieve? Pushing a performer to do something before she's ready can be extremely dangerous. I'll know when Mandy's ready to include the move in her act. And Mandy will know it too. Coaching Mandy is my job, Genevieve. You've made some good artistic suggestions, and I'm sure Mandy appreciates your input."

"I do," I say, only now I'm starting to wonder if all along Genevieve has been trying to push me into doing something dangerous. Didn't she try to talk me into climbing the maple tree?

Genevieve crosses her arms over her chest. “I was just trying to help Mandy. I want her performance to pop.”

Maybe it’s the speed at which Genevieve is speaking or the fact she’s not looking at Terence or me, but I suddenly understand, even if Genevieve can’t see it herself, that a part of her would enjoy seeing me screw up.

I could be angry. What if Terence hadn’t been around and Genevieve had pushed me to do the move before I was ready? What if I’d had an accident? What if I’d climbed the maple tree with Leo and gotten kicked out of circus camp too?

I could be angry, but I’m not. The feeling I have takes me a little by surprise.

I actually feel bad for Genevieve.

That’s because I know exactly what she is feeling. Haven’t I felt the same way about her?

Twenty-One

Our final performance starts at four in the afternoon.

With so much to do before then, I expect the rest of the day to fly, but it doesn't. It crawls.

Before lunch, we pack. Then we strip our beds and leave the blankets, sheets and pillowcases in a pile on the dorm floor.

Hana makes me promise to Skype her once a week. "That way," she says, "I can see you and also practice English."

"Hey, what about my Korean lessons?" I say. "So far, all I know is *pal-kkum-chi* and *boricha* and...what's the name of that flower on your back again?"

"*Mugunghwa*," Hana says. "But please do not say anything about tattoos to my parents when you meet them."

Suzanne has given me permission to skip flex class and juggling so I can keep working on my star rolls with Terence. Genevieve won't be in la palestre with us. When she tells me Suzanne needs her help putting together the program for this afternoon, I wonder if it was Terence's idea. I think he wants a break from Genevieve.

We spend the first half hour reviewing my double and triple star rolls. After I do two triple star rolls in a row without making a single mistake, I look at Terence. Before I even open my mouth, he gives me the answer to the question I was about to ask. "Maybe," he says.

Everything about circus camp feels different this afternoon. Partly it's because the building is so much quieter without Leo and Guillaume's laughter. Partly it's because we all know circus camp is almost over. Though most of us have only known each other for two weeks, it's hard to imagine not being together anymore. And, of course, things feel different because we're excited—and nervous—about today's performance.

At lunchtime Suzanne comes to the cafeteria to make a few final announcements. She reads them from a list. "As you all know," she says, looking up from her sheet, "Leo has been sent home to Brussels. Like all of you, he was warned about breaking camp rules. Though we consider what he did a serious offense, it is his first, and I thought I'd let you all know, since Leo is your friend and I know you care about him, that his application to MCC will still be considered."

Guillaume jumps up from his seat, slaps his thigh and calls out, "Yesss!"

Suzanne continues reading. "I also want to let you know I had an email this morning from Anastasia. Her father's condition has stabilized, and she asked me to wish all of you good luck this afternoon. There will be a short reception after your performance. If your parents are here, be sure to invite them. Dormitories must be vacated by six. Good luck to all of you this afternoon. I hope I'll see some of you at circus camp next year—or in the building, if you come back to attend MCC."

I get shivers when Suzanne says that. I know my chances of being accepted into MCC are better now that Genevieve is injured. But if I'm accepted, will I be able to talk my parents into letting me move to Montreal and do high school here? I think my mom would say yes. But would my dad come around?

When I'm putting away my tray, Suzanne taps my shoulder. "I need to speak to you privately, Mandy."

"Is something wrong?" I'm remembering how Suzanne needed to talk to Anastasia privately after her father's heart attack. "Is it my dad?" It's the first question that pops into my mind.

"Everyone's fine," Suzanne assures me. "But your mother's plane has been delayed. She telephoned my office just now from the Vancouver airport. She was hoping we could delay the performance until she got here, but I explained that that was impossible. I'm sorry, Mandy."

I tell myself I'm not the only one whose parents won't be at the performance. Guillaume's parents live too far away to make the trip, and it's too expensive for Genevieve's parents.

* * *

After lunch, it's back to la palestre. Terence and I have another forty minutes to work together. Halfway through our session, he looks at me and says, "Okay."

I'm confused. "Okay?"

"Okay, I'm thinking I might let you do the triple star roll this afternoon. Once—for your finale. *To make it pop.* You've been doing so well and working so hard. But only if you think you're ready for it."

I take a deep breath. "I'm ready."

"Just make sure you keep your back straight."

After that, the time does fly. In fact, now it's going too quickly. I only get to practice the move twice more because the riggers need to set up la palestre for the show. There are metal folding chairs in every corner of the room. It will be a three-ring circus, a tribute to the old circus tradition. Throughout our performance, there will be three separate acts for the audience to follow.

There is only time for a hurried rehearsal. Outside la palestre, relatives and friends gather for the show. We can hear the excited hum of conversations. Gillian, the flexibility coach, is wearing a whistle around her neck, and when she blows it, we follow her out the back door of la palestre to the equipment room. We'll be back in ten minutes, after the audience is seated.

When we hear the first chords of "Gonna Fly Now," the theme song to *Rocky*, it's our cue that the show is about to begin. We form a line and jog back into la palestre. I can feel the music filling me up. Soon I'll be doing the triple star roll, which is about as close as I've ever come to flying. If only Mom could be here to see me do it!

Those of us not performing in the first act move to the back. Guillaume is doing the phone-call routine Genevieve and I saw Leo do at the beginning of circus camp. Genevieve is sitting up at the front, near the rope and tissu. I catch her eye, and she nods at me.

Guillaume pretends to telephone an older lady who is sitting in a chair near him. When he blows the woman a kiss and she blushes and covers her mouth with her hand, the audience cracks up.

Guillaume saunters over to the lady and sits down in her lap. He's slipping his arm around her shoulder when he notices the man sitting in the next chair—it must be her husband.

Guillaume lifts his hands into the air so the audience can see them trembling. He pops up from the lady's lap and slinks away in the direction of the equipment room. On his way he pauses, catches the lady's eye, takes out his pretend phone and calls her again. From the way he grins, we can all tell he's trying to arrange a date to see her later. He puts the phone back into his pocket, winks at the audience and disappears.

There's more laughter from the audience and applause too.

Hana and two other girls are on the mats, doing the pretzel. Hana's feet are over her head, and I can see right into her eyes. She looks at me without blinking, and when she smiles, I know her smile is for the whole audience, not just me. Hana might have been homesick, and her English still needs work, but I'm beginning to understand that she has what it takes to become a circus star. Sure, she's hardworking and talented. But she's got courage too.

I'm waiting by the rope when I hear Carly Simon's voice begin to sing "Itsy Bitsy Spider."

The riggers have just finished arranging the flowerpots and garden hose. I don't know why, but I'm not nervous. Maybe it's because my mom's not here. Except for the friends I've made at circus camp, no one in the audience knows me. *If I screw up*...I stop myself. I'm not planning to screw up.

I'm excited. I'm ready.

I've practiced hard and long, and I want to share what I've learned at circus camp. I want to show the audience what I can do—and how much I love my rope.

My arms and legs work together as I climb. I feel strong, confident. My act is becoming automatic, the way Terence told me it would if I practiced hard enough.

The audience lets out an appreciative *aah* when I do my single star roll. Wait, I think, until you see my triple.

I'm working and I'm playing. And now, already—how did the time go so quickly?—it's nearly the end of my act and time for my triple star roll.

I climb nearly to the ceiling of la palestre and gaze out at the audience beneath me. Genevieve is in the first row. Her injured leg is elevated on a chair, and she is craning her neck to watch me. Terence must be there too.

I take a deep breath and prepare to invert. The rope is hanging on my right side. I concentrate as I wrap it over my right thigh, then three times around my waist. I tug on it to make sure it's secure. I look up at the carabiner. When I do, I think of Louise.

This time, though, thinking of her doesn't make me feel afraid. Louise died a terrible, senseless death, but she died doing what she loved. I am lucky to be able to do what I love too. If one day I make it and become a professional aerialist, I won't climb only for myself or for the audience. I'll climb for Louise too.

I take another look down at the audience. Why is Genevieve waving her hands? My first thought is that she's trying to distract me. Trying to ruin my performance. *How dare she do that?*

I look up and away from Genevieve. I can't let her rattle me.

I hook my toe on the rope. I can almost hear Terence's voice in my ear, telling me, "Release! Now!"

But I don't. Something stops me.

That's exactly when I realize what I've done. I've wrapped the rope over the wrong thigh. And now I can see Terence waving at me too. They both know that if I let go now, the rope will set me on the wrong side. I won't be able to move at all. I'll be trapped in the air like some dumb bug caught in a spider's web.

Carly Simon is singing, *"Down came the rain and washed the spider out..."*

There's just enough time to make the fix. My fingers are shaking, but I manage to loosen the rope from around my thigh. When I wrap it around my left thigh and then three times around my waist, I start feeling more like a spider again. I hook my toe, and as I release it from the rope, all I can think is, Thank you, Genevieve!

When I dangle in the air, and when I slide down to the mats, the audience is clapping. Except for Genevieve and Terence, no one else seems to realize how close I came to screwing up my finale.

A few people are actually standing up and giving me an ovation. I feel proud and embarrassed at the same time, but I take a bow.

Only when I'm lifting my head and looking at the people who have stood up do I realize who is in the audience.. My mom. She must have caught another plane. How else could she have made it to the performance on time? I feel myself starting to tear up. Not only because my mom just saw me do a triple star roll at the MCC, but because my dad did too. He is standing next to her, clapping his hands.

I can't hug them until the reception, which is being held out on the terrace.

When I get there, I spot my parents talking to a distinguished-looking Korean couple. Hana's parents.

I expect Hana to rush to them, but she walks over calmly. "We are so proud of you," they tell her, and then they kiss her.

Hana's *mugunghwa* tattoo is covered by her leotard. I wonder if she will show the tattoo to her parents when she is back in Korea, or if she will continue to keep it a secret.

"Mom! Dad! You made it in time! Dad, I didn't know you were coming." My voice breaks a little.

"He decided at the last minute," my mom says. "When he saw me packing my suitcase, he got on the computer and booked another ticket."

Mom won't stop hugging me. On another day I might feel embarrassed, but not today. "You were amazing," she says. "You never told me you were practicing the triple star roll."

Dad is watching us. "I nearly screwed up that last move," I tell him. "I was about to make a really dumb mistake—"

"But you fixed it," he says. "I saw you adjusting the rope up there, so I figured something must've gone wrong. You made a mistake. It happens." He's watching my face. "But you fixed it. That's what's important. Fixing things. I'm proud of you, Mandy."

Dad is hugging me now too.

Hana taps my shoulder. "I want you to meet my mother and father, please," she says. And then I spot Genevieve hobbling toward us.

This reception is starting to feel like another three-ring circus.

I want to hang out with my mom and dad, and I want to meet Hana's parents, but first I need to talk to Genevieve. I tell Hana and my parents I'll be right back, and I walk toward her. I've never seen anyone get around as quickly on crutches as she does. Something tells me she'll be back on the tissu sooner than anyone expects.

"Hey," I say to her. "Thanks for what you did. You saved me from looking like a total idiot out there."

"That would have been something, wouldn't it?" Genevieve says. Her eyes are dancing. I think she's picturing me trapped in my rope. "Anyway, you don't have to thank me. You'd have done the same thing for me."

I nod my head. It's too hard for me to speak. I think the reason I'm getting all emotional is that this time, Genevieve is right.

I would have done the same thing for her.

Acknowledgments

I could never have written this book without the help of many people. Special thanks to two colleagues at Marianopolis College, Philip Dann and Kate Sheckler, who introduced me to their friends at Montreal's École nationale de cirque. One of those friends was Selene Ballesteros-Minguer, who got me hooked on the world of rope climbing. ENC administrators Daniela Arendasova, Laurence Cardin, Marilou Cousineau and Christophe Rousseau gave me access to the facility. Librarian Anna-Karyna Barlati made me feel at home in her library. Kia-Melinda Eastman helped me learn about tissu. Aaron Marquise, my favorite clown in Montreal, kept me entertained and taught me that intelligence is a big part of clowning. Summer circus camp students Ainsleigh Jackson, Elodie Paquin and Ryan Madis answered my questions and demonstrated their routines. Aerial instructor Sarah Poole patiently answered many questions and reviewed sections of the manuscript.

Thanks also to the entire team at Orca Book Publishers, especially to Robin Stevenson for her gentle, incisive input. Thank you to aerialist Adrienne Jack-Sands and photographer Ibon Landa for the stunning cover image.

And, as always, thanks to my husband, Michael Shenker, and my daughter, Alicia Melamed, for their love and support and for letting me talk out another story with them. All of you have shown me that when the stars align, work can feel like play.

This is MONIQUE POLAK's seventeenth novel for young adults. Her historical novel *What World Is Left* won the 2009 Quebec Writers' Federation Prize for Children's and Young Adult Literature. Monique is also a journalist whose work appears regularly in the Montreal *Gazette* and in Postmedia publications across Canada. She has been teaching English literature and humanities at Marianopolis College in Montreal, Quebec, for thirty years. Monique lives in Montreal with her husband.

When all the world's a stage.

LOOKING FOR MORE?

Check out:

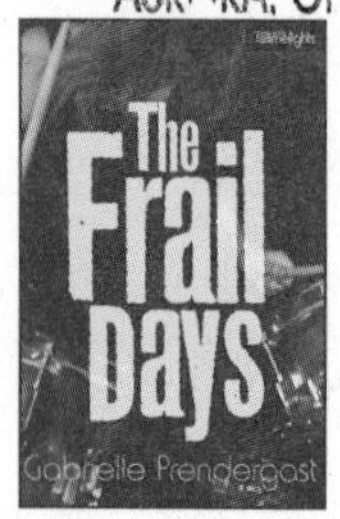

9781459804654 PB
9781459804661 EPUB

9781459805798 PB
9781459805811 EPUB

9781459804319 PB
9781459804333 EPUB

9781459804289 PB
9781459804302 EPUB

9781459804616 PB
9781459804630 EPUB

9781459802803 PB
9781459802827 EPUB

9781459806450 PB
9781459806290 EPUB

9781459804135 PB
9781459804159 EPUB

www.orcalimelights.com

AVAILABLE AS EBOOKS

ORCA BOOK PUBLISHERS
www.orcabook.com • 1-800-210-5277